MW01680843

Reasons Why I Am a Unitarian

Anatiposi

John Beard

Reasons Why I Am a Unitarian

Reprint of the original, first published in 1872.

1st Edition 2023 | ISBN: 978-3-38213-348-1

Anatiposi Verlag is an imprint of Outlook Verlagsgesellschaft mbH.

Verlag (Publisher): Outlook Verlag GmbH, Zeilweg 44, 60439 Frankfurt, Deutschland
Vertretungsberechtigt (Authorized to represent): E. Roepke, Zeilweg 44, 60439 Frankfurt, Deutschland
Druck (Print): Books on Demand GmbH, In de Tarpen 42, 22848 Norderstedt, Deutschland

REASONS
WHY I AM A UNITARIAN.

LONDON:
PRINTED BY WOODFALL AND KINDER,
MILFORD LANE, STRAND, W.C.

REASONS

WHY I AM A UNITARIAN,

IN

A SERIES OF LETTERS TO A FRIEND.

BY

JOHN R. BEARD, D.D.

Third Edition, revised.

This Truth, more beautiful than all beside—
That He whose name is Love, and from whose heart,
As from a living and immortal root,
The whole fair universe hath budded forth,
Hath granted us the high and holy right
To call Him FATHER. So all things speak
God's Fatherhood and the Brotherhood of man.

LONDON:
BRITISH AND FOREIGN UNITARIAN ASSOCIATION,
178, STRAND, W.C.
1872.

TO

IVIE MACKIE, ESQ.,

THIRD TIME

MAYOR OF MANCHESTER.

MY DEAR SIR,

The manliness with which you avow, the earnestness with which you support, and the fidelity with which you exemplify the simple, sublime, and most salutary religion of Jesus, the Light and Saviour of the world, must be my apology for inscribing your name on this inconsiderable page. Bear with me if, in addition, I thus publicly acknowledge the generous aid with which you have encouraged my humble endeavours to make the press a channel for extending the benign influence of Unitarianism—equally dear to us both.

I remain, my dear Sir, with high respect and kind regards,

Your Pastor and Friend,

JOHN R. BEARD.

2, CAMP TERRACE, NEAR MANCHESTER,
December 14*th*, 1859.

TABLE OF CONTENTS.

PREFACE.

THE present time is especially favourable for a wise and earnest effort to offer a purer form of Christianity to the large, various, and important class which we call *The People*. Never before, within my experience—an experience extending over more than the third of a century—has there been any approach to the same freedom from the taint of infidelity, the same sense of moral and spiritual want, the same earnest desire of religious light, the same earnestness of inquiry "Who will show us any good?" or the same degree of preparation in mental culture and general enlightenment. By no means, indeed, are these desirable qualities, either in themselves or in the extent of their general prevalence, all that the friends of the simple Gospel could wish. They are, however, every day growing and extending, while already, they suffice to open the ear of multitudes, who hitherto have remained deaf, to a religious revival in which reason and Scripture are to be honoured, rather than passion. In consequence, opportunities of exercising their proper religious influence are offered to

Unitarian ministers throughout the land, and especially in our large city populations. If these opportunities are wisely profited by, a large reward may be expected from the hand of the heavenly Father. The needful wisdom involves, it is submitted, two things—first, a going-forth to the people; and second, an offer of the Gospel, and nothing but the Gospel, both positively and distinctively. There must be a going-forth. Pulpit ministrations no longer suffice. The Christian minister must become a missionary. Like his professed Master, he must "go about doing good." In going forth into social life, he may act in various ways for the improvement of his fellow-men; but he must not fail to preach to them "the unsearchable riches of Christ." In order that those riches may be clearly seen, intelligently apprehended, and duly valued, they must be set forth distinctively. But this positive and distinctive teaching can have little effect, unless it proceed from a heart deeply sensible of its value, and be emphatically directed so as to promote the great aim of the Gospel in the renewal as well as enrichment of the life. No propagandism can be truly Christian, or perform a Christian work, which springs not from "the life of God in the soul of man," and aims not to form individuals anew after the image of the Saviour. Nothing short of this deserves the name of Christian endeavour; nothing short of this can be expected to secure the coöperation of God's Spirit, and to receive the Divine blessing. No mere change of opinion is *the* change which God designs, and which Christ came to effect. It is with the heart that man believeth unto righteousness, while it is with the tongue that confession is made unto salvation. (Rom. x. 10.) True religious reform ends, if it does not begin, with the affections. In his affections is every man's life. Until the affections are filled with the spirit of Christ, the work of religion is at the best in only rudimental and preparatory stages. One of these stages is connected with the rectification of theological falsities. The process is highly important. "Acquaint now thyself with God, and be at peace," says Eliphaz, in the Book of Job (xxii. 21); and certain it is, that the good of which he speaks cannot come to any one until he is led by the Son to the Father (John xiv. 6), for in the God and Father of Jesus alone is to be found absolute love combined with absolute wisdom and power. A clear utterance then must there be, as for the truth of God, so against human corruptions. The religion of the Bible must be substituted for the theologies of the Church. Where the attempt is made by that living tongue which is inspired by a soul living in the Divine truth, of which Christ is to us the reservoir and the source, good must ensue—good invaluable as well as large and various.

Happy the men who are called by Divine Providence to achieve so good a result. Such men are found in the Unitarian body. The number of such men is daily increasing; yet the work increases more rapidly. Need is there to pray the Lord of the harvest to send more labourers into his harvest.

The need is great and urgent. Thousands are without Christ, if not without God; thousands live scarcely more than a mere worldly life; thousands vegetate in religious ignorance and unconcern; thousands sink daily deeper and deeper in sin; thousands perish in vice;—again, other thousands are all but ready to renounce popular forms of Christianity, or pine and groan under the burdens they impose;—to all of whom Unitarianism could minister beneficially, and might minister acceptably, if only heralds of the grace of God appeared in sufficient number, and instinct with the right spirit. May the Giver of every good and perfect gift pour out a full effusion of the spirit of his Son on our Unitarian churches, and make them each a fountain whence the waters of life shall flow forth on their respective neighbourhoods in copious and refreshing streams! A hope to contribute somewhat toward so desirable a result, has animated the writer in publishing the following pages, which he now solemnly commends to the blessing of the God and Father of the Lord Jesus Christ.

WHY AM I A UNITARIAN?

LETTER I.—INTRODUCTORY.

My Dear Edward,—The surprise that you express at my being a Unitarian is not altogether without a reason. You have been brought up in the orthodox system,—you have been taught to avoid free discussion,—you have been led to believe that your eternal safety depends on your holding the orthodox opinions,—you have been imbued with the feeling that Unitarianism is the high road to perdition, and that Unitarians are little if anything else than deists, and so you have come to look with pity, if not dislike, on Unitarians, and to wonder how it is that I can be a Unitarian. To one of your ingenuous nature the feeling must, I am sure, be painful, and I can well understand how you came to write your letter inquiring, Why I am a Unitarian? The question deserves an answer, if only because it seems to imply a disposition on your part to look a little into the grounds and reasons of Unitarianism. Such a disposition I cordially approve. It is your duty to examine the ground on which you stand, and that you cannot do honestly and fully unless you examine the ground on which I stand. Our relationship has shown you the existence of a form of Christianity in which much of what you consider fundamental is disowned, and disowned by persons whom you esteem and respect, and who, you have reason to think, are not without means of forming a sound judgment,—whose lives are at least as good as their neighbours', and whose disinterestedness you cannot call into question.

In such circumstances you act naturally in asking me a reason of the hope that is in me, only I beg of you, do not shrink from giving an attentive ear to what I shall lay before you. Religion is too serious a matter to be dealt with slightly. As you will have to answer for the result to God, and will assuredly feel the consequences of the result throughout the whole of your existence, so ought you to be very careful every step you take, and when, as now, you have once begun, take all possible pains to proceed wisely. But as in all investigations, so especially in this, wisdom demands thoroughness, you had better not begin if you doubt your strength to persevere. You will not infer from these words that I am about to trouble you at length in this matter, important though it is. Excellent works exist already, in the pages of which you may study, in all their details, the questions at issue between Trinitarians and Unitarians. A list of some of these I will append to my letters. My object is simply to lay before you, in a concise form, some general reasons which, serving as an answer to your question, "Why are you a Unitarian?" may at least prove to you that I have not, to use your own words, "left the good old paths" without cause. Had those paths appeared to me good, I should have continued to walk therein. Did they now appear to me good, I would instantly return to them. If I have turned aside from them, it is because the hand of Providence has led me to "a more excellent way." Where God calls me I dare not refuse to go. Where God bids me stay I must remain. Not lightly have I acted in espousing Unitarianism. Young though you are, you know enough of my history to be aware that I have enjoyed advantages for the study of religious matters. I have arrived at a time of life when the judgment has some maturity, and when the outlook into eternity may well make a man cautious, reverent, and anxious to be right. Had my temporal interests been with me paramount, I should not be where I am. I do not pretend to be free from occasions of error, but at least I have striven to know the truth. For during a great portion of my life, not a year has passed but I have reviewed the foundations on which I stand, nor does a day now pass without witnessing some effort on my part to learn more clearly and more fully what is the mind and will of God. If, under these circumstances, I have failed, I trust for acceptance to the mercy of the Heavenly Father, assured that what he requires is not so much that his children should absolutely see as he sees, but that they should try to make his views of eternal realities theirs. In this assurance I can conscientiously ask you to follow me in the considerations I am about to submit to your notice. May God make and keep you honest, sincere, earnest,—desirous to know, willing to receive, and ready to profess the truth which, in his Providence, he may set before your mind! Only do not commit the gross mistake of thinking that any truth can become your truth by adoption. Aid you may derive from other men, but truth can become yours only by careful inquiry and meditation on your own part, and for your own instruction. Nor can religious truth be obtained by any mere intellectual process. If you would know God, you must worship, love, and serve God. If you would know Christ, you must sit reverently at his feet, and, like him, go about doing good. If you would possess God's Spirit, you must not only pray for it, but be careful to cherish it within you and manifest it around you. An hour of childlike obedience to your Heavenly Father will do more to open your eyes than a year's reading in books of divinity.

Yours truly,

JOHN R. BEARD.

LETTER II.—WHAT IS UNITARIANISM?

My Dear Edward,—I cannot tell you why I am a Unitarian, unless you know what Unitarianism is. On this point you must allow me to say that your knowledge is both erroneous and defective. Your views are not, indeed, so grossly false as the veiws entertained by many. To much of what you have heard you have not given credit. Your general intelligence has, in a measure, preserved you from misjudgments, and the fairness of your mind and the simplicity of your character have made you at least hope better things than have come to your ears. The dark hues borne by some statements have produced in you the opposite to their intended effect, and put you on making a formal inquiry as to my reasons for being a Unitarian. Yet are you not free from misapprehensions, and will therefore, I hope, give heed to what I have to say on this preliminary question.

The question divides itself into two branches—first, What is Unitarianism as held by me? and, What is Unitarianism as held by others? Regard to exact truth induces me to put the matter thus. I do not wish to pledge any one to the views I entertain, but equally I cannot undertake to espouse or defend the views which others entertain, unless they agree with my own. The distinction implies diversity, and some diversity doubtless exists. The diversity for the most part regards two things,—first, the methods of proof; second, the results. The methods of proof vary in this, that some Unitarians give prominence to internal evidences, others to external, while some, again, combine the two, holding that the two are consistent views. For instance,—here is one Unitarian minister who dwells mostly on the essential truth and beauty of the life of Christ, and holds that life to be, under God, the source of life to every believer. Here is another, who dwells mostly on the words of Christ, as truth attested by the miracles which he wrought, and the recorded effects of the Gospel when preached to the world. A third, however, regards the words of Christ as one manifestation of his divine life, and the miracles as another, and finds a third in the beneficial working of the Gospel in society. Following different paths, all three are led to acknowledge in Christ divine wisdom and divine power, and so to receive him as God's ambassador and representative. This result, however, is not unattended with diversity, for here is one person who preferably calls Christ "a teacher sent from God," and there another, to whom he appears as in the truest and deepest sense, "the Saviour of the world." Nevertheless, the former maintains, as strenuously as the latter, that his trust is in God, and not in man. So, in relation to the person of Christ, diversities prevail. One class of Unitarians, influenced by scriptural statements in which they see disclosures respecting his nature, hold that Christ existed before he was born of Mary, and in a personal form was God's instrument in the creation of the world. In this class there are persons who ascribe to Christ some share in the divine essence, and accordingly apply to him the epithet God in a secondary sense. Another class, equally influenced by scriptural statements, in which they see disclosures respecting his nature, hold that Christ had no existence before he was born of Mary, and was simply a human teacher, who, with God's ever present aid, lived a holy life, and died in the discharge of his duty. These two diversities, wide apart as they seem to stand, have a point of union in the divine element which both acknowledge in Christ. A third class, not less influenced by Scripture, but taking as their guide, not so much the letter as the spirit of the Bible, not so much particular epithets as its general tenor, and proceeding on the principle that its aim is not to teach metaphysics, nor to disclose and define modes and orders of being, but to reveal spiritual realities, to make fatherly will known to man, to plant God's own spirit in man's mind, so as to win man's heart to God, and make man himself one with God in act as well as thought, have been led to find in the scriptural Christ the true and full manifestation of God in Jesus of Nazareth, the Son of God, who, in virtue of his perfect obedience to his Heavenly Father, was raised into most intimate and ceaseless communion with that Father, and so received from him the fountain of life, the plenitude of the Divine Spirit, in virtue of which he spoke God's words, and accomplished God's will. This third view connects itself with the two preceding ones in the recognition of the divine in Christ, while it sees in that divine element something acquired by, and so truly inherent in Christ, and that something as nothing less than God's own given Spirit. Yet here a limit is acknowledged, for the view owns the proper humanity of Christ, and so adds that Christ pessessed the Spirit of God as largely and as fully as that Spirit could be possessed by a perfect man. If I mention a fourth class, I shall probably exhaust the subject, and give the view taken by the greater number. It is this—God was in Christ reconciling himself to the world, and, in consequence, Christ is the Saviour of the world. Those who belong to this class are content with what to them are facts, without speculating about the exact nature of those facts. Religion, they think, is for living rather than for thinking. The Bible they hold to be the book of life, and not a book for disputation. God, in their belief, makes his character known by various means, and supereminently by and in Jesus Christ, in order to teach men the way to himself, rather than to decide questions of dark import and doubtful issue. Content with humbly striving to know, to do, and to bear God's will under the light and aid given by Christ, they are not bent on penetrating into sacred things which they consider unrevealed, but think that to love and serve God and man after the manner and in the power of Christ, is the true and sure way to God here and hereafter. The practical character of this fourth class presents the point at which they are one with the other classes, for all Unitarians hold that the essence of the Gospel is Christ-like love.

In this grand acknowledgment they are, of necessity, united, because they are united in the acknowledgment of two other fundamental verities, namely that "there is one God, and none other but he" (Mark xii. 32), who is verily the Father of his intelligent creatures, and that the Gospel, from first to last, is a manifestation of that love. As there is but one God the Father, so are they agreed that "the Son of God" is not "God the Son." And as "the Father sent the Son to be the Saviour of the world," so is the Son the gift, and not the cause, of the Father's love. Consequently, salvation is properly of grace and not of purchase, and redemption is unprompted and unconditioned rescue, and not the satisfaction either of God himself or God's law. Yet is this not to be understood as if sin were tolerated by the Heavenly Father. A wise and good earthly father is, even from his wisdom and goodness, unable to endure disobedience; and the Heavenly Father, who is absolutely good, must by all possible means ensure the triumph and prevalence of goodness. Sin, in consequence, must be destroyed;—but the sinner may be saved, "even though as by fire." In a word, God, as the universal Father, aims at universal good, and so makes his dealings corrective, remedial, and restorative. It is not that he punishes the less, but that he punishes with effect, and he punishes with that effect which a father cannot, as a father, help entertaining, cherishing, and pursuing. But an Almighty Father must succeed in the ends he proposes to himself, else he is not Almighty. The partial prevalence of evil in the final issue, not only robs God of his paternal character, but, if it does not dethrone the deity, places another divinity by his side, almost as powerful as, if not more powerful than, himself. If this is true, then, the time will never come when Christ shall have subdued all things to himself, and God be all in all (1 Cor. xv. 24, *seq.*). The unity of God, the essential goodness of God, the consequent brotherhood of man, a real and effectual salvation through Christ, the Son of man and the Son of God—these are the grand truths in which consists the unity of the Unitarian Church. Here is "the one faith, one hope, one God and Father of all, who is above all, and one Lord Jesus Christ, who is Lord of all" (Acts x. 36), in the acknowledgment of whom, through "the one spirit" of God in Christ, Unitarians are "one spiritual body built upon the foundation of the apostles and prophets, Jesus Christ himself being the chief corner stone" (1 Cor. viii. 6, *seq.*; Ephes. ii. 20; iv. 3), which is "the Church of the living God, the pillar and ground of the truth" (1 Tim. iii. 16), the rather because admitting diversities of gifts, but the same spirit; differences of administrations, but the same Lord; diversities of operations, but the same God working all in all (1 Cor. xii. 4, *seq.*); we endeavour to keep the unity of the spirit in the bond of peace (Ephes. iv. 3), and not in the rigours and strifes of an unattainable and undesirable identity of opinion (Rom. xiv.). Here, too, is the link by which my own view becomes one with the view of the Unitarian Church in general, only I leave to every one the right which I enjoy and exercise myself of professing his faith in words of his own choosing. The statements I have made will show you that, in general, the diversities existing among Unitarians regard little else than the form. I believe that the following propositions would be generally acknowledged by them as comprising the fundamentals of the Gospel :—

1. There is one God, the Father, and none other but he.

2. There is one Lord Jesus Christ, who came, divinely empowered, to lead men to duty and to God.

3. There is one Spirit of God, comforting and sanctifying all Christ's faithful disciples.

4. There is one true Church, comprising all, of every denomination, who live holily in Christ Jesus.

5. There is one bond of Christian unity, the bond of peace, and therefore the bond of mutual toleration.

6. There is one final abode for the spirits of just men made perfect, the home of the Heavenly Father.

These six points, reduced to their simplest elements, present a fatherly God, and a brotherly Lord, as the essential articles of Unitarian Christianity. At least in this ultimate form you may be assured you have the one universal faith of Unitarianism. The God who made the world reveals himself through Jesus, in order to destroy evil, and bring all men in holiness and true happiness to himself. Such is my faith and hope, and such is the faith and hope of every Unitarian. More than this some Unitarians may profess; with less than this I do not see how any one can take the Unitarian name. Here, however, I desire to be cautious; for I wish not to judge my brother. "Let every man be fully persuaded in his own mind" (Rom. xiv. 5); for whatsoever is not of such persuasion is sin (23).

I must not pass from the present point without expressly directing your attention to an important fact. The view which

I have given as constituting Unitarianism is a view which Unitarians have not made, but found. In other words, this is their view of the Gospel. My religion comes from God. As I receive it from no brother man, so I have not devised it myself. To me religion is, from first to last, a revelation. By revelation God has made himself known to me. By revelation God has made Christ known to me. By revelation God speaks to me in my daily life. The Gospel is emphatically *the* revelation of God to man through the Son of man. All divine truth is from above, being from "the Father of lights," "from whom cometh down every good and perfect gift." Man can no more invent religion than he can make good evil or evil good. Religion is grounded on the eternal laws of spiritual reality, of which God is the centre and the source. Religion is consequently God's will made known to man. Nay, rather it is God himself made known to man; it is the spirit of the Everlasting Father disclosed to our human spirits, that in the light we may find power and peace. That divine reality, variously set forth and richly communicated, also evidencing itself even as the light of day, or the comfort of home, I find concentrated in the Gospel, whose focal point is Christ. In consequence, the Gospel is my religion. That is, the view which, under God's providence, I have been led to take of the Gospel is my religion. That view is essentially a Unitarian view, for it owns but one God, who makes himself known through Jesus Christ. Unitarianism, then, is to me no man-made system. Were it so, I would discard it from this hour. It is no tradition handed down from ancient creed-makers. In such a reed I could not place my trust. It is no aggregate of human opinions, but a divinely-given blessing, attesting its divinity by its correspondence with all I am, all I know, and all I want.

In this statement I have properly confined myself to the

central ideas of Unitarianism, because I wished to show it to you in its simplest form. It may however, be desirable to develope these primitive truths in one or two ways. And first, the idea of God. In every form of religion the idea of God contains the entire religion itself. So the whole of true religion, or religion in its highest form, is contained in its idea of God. When, then, God is said to be one, it is also said that properly there is no other God. Thus you see that the religion of the Bible is a monotheism. In being a monotheism, that religion takes its station at the head of all the highest forms of religion in the world, and corresponds with the best thought of the greatest philosophers on the subject. It further carries us back to the most ancient ideas of civilized nations, for behind all polytheistic forms of religion, at least as they are now, there lies the grand recognition of one God, the infinite source of all things and all beings. You thus see that in its central truth, the Bible contains the religion of civilization, and so, in regard to numbers as well as dignity, stands at the head of the religions of the world. A truth thus acknowledged, belongs to the great heritage of the human mind. As such, its sources must be co-eval and co-extensive with human culture. Where can such a source be found unless in the Deity himself? Here the God who made the human race is its instructor, and religion is the one great revelation. The channel through which that revelation was made must partake of the universality of its source. That channel is the universe of mind and matter, or God unveiling himself in the creatures he has made. In other words, God's Spirit stamps an image of itself on man's spirit through the impressive action of the sun, moon, and stars, the interchanges of day and night, the recurrence of the seasons, nor least, the varied discipline and genial influences of human society, especially the home.

The religious impressions thus produced, find utterance,

under God's inspiration, from the lips of eminent sages, whose words, gathered and treasured up, are communicated by the father to the son, and so pass from generation to generation. In the course of time they take form and pressure in certain external signs. It may be in a grand hieroglyph. It may be in a series of symbolic paintings. It may be in symbolic sculptures. It may be in symbolic edifices. At length an Abraham, a Moses, a David, is born, and by their prophetic tongue, and the cunning of their interpreting hand, they take a written shape, and so become the first great prolific germs of a religion with written records. Hence the Bible. No sooner is the essence of religion consigned to the custody of writing than a new and brighter era begins. The Decalogue, written by God's Spirit with the fingers of Moses, became the corner-stone of Hebrewism, and Hebrewism is the parent of Christianity. Thus, in addition to other channels of communication, God now speaks with his children through the great thoughts and gread deeds of his prophets, and so prepares the way for the final revelation of himself, in Jesus Christ his Son. Here, again, begins a new, fuller, and more varied, as well as brighter and more benign, series of self-disclosures on the part of God, which, continued under the direct influence of his Spirit, passes from age to age, through apostles, martyrs, confessors, and holy men and women, down to the present hour.

You thus see that revelation is of two kinds—first, special; and second, general. It is special in degree in all the great servants of God. It is general in all who resemble those servants in loving obedience, though the resemblance be even small. God never left, and never leaves, himself without a witness. You also see that the Bible is the great record of God's dealings with men in their religious relations to him and to one another.

You may also learn that Jesus stands midway between the

old civilization and the new, being the point toward which all previous influences tended, and the point from which all after influences flowed. It may be added that, as he is, under God, the fountain Head, whence all now comes, so is he the great ocean whither they all flow, and where they will find their fulness and their rest. Of the manner in which that rest will be secured, the revelation of God as the Father of human-kind, and especially as the Father of Jesus, tells us all we can either know or need. It tells us first, as we are told in the New Testament, that Jesus, as God's Son, made obedience to God the spring of his glory, and the source of his influence. Looking toward God, Jesus was a learner and a worshipper. Looking toward man, Jesus communicates of the light and power he so receives. Whatever Jesus did, he did all in obedience to the will of God. Whatever Jesus imparts, he imparts all as the medium of God's grace to man.

These facts stand out clear and prominent in the pages of the Bible. They are, also, deeply stamped on the history of the last eighteen centuries. Moreover, they are consonant with the experience of every true Christian disciple.

This being so, all other matters are of minor importance. We may or we may not be able—we may be more or less unable—to explain *the manner* in which God bestows light and salvation on men through his Son. The question of, How? always difficult, is specially difficult in religion. In religion, indeed, the inquiry baffles our most searching endeavours, Yet—such is man's folly—we turn away from the great facts or certainties of the gospel, to questions touching the things which God has left hidden, and even go so far in our infatuation as to make our own opinions on these points the touchstone of orthodoxy and the shibboleth of salvation. Nevertheless the thoughtful few are beginning to open their eyes. Having studied the history of the Church, they see that, like all mere human notions, the opinions that councils, synods, and conferences have sanctioned as divine truths, have changed from the first, and are changing still; so that no two ages, scarcely any two authorities, have agreed, or do precisely agree, respecting original sin, the trinity, the atonement. At the utmost, the fancied agreement is in the letter. The moment you attempt to translate the letter into thought, or to set it forth in the shape of any known reality, you call forth dissent, and that dissent is as various as the minds occupied with the subject.

It is characteristic of Unitarianism to make little of these variations of human opinion, which are no more than the reflex images of individual peculiarities of temperament, desire, speculation, or aim; which are the offspring of tendencies of thought, or schools of philosophy; which are sparks from the anvil of constructors of logical systems of theology. Failing to behold the light of divine truth in these traditions of men, Unitarianism renounces them, and fixes its gaze, in reverence and love, on the eternal and unfading truth of the one God the Father, and the one Lord Jesus Christ, and the one gift of grace made by the Father through the Son, attested and made operative by the Spirit. This, at least, is what I do, and this would I advise you to do.

Thus far, in my own words, have I told you what Unitarianism is. I have given you my view of Unitarianism. That you may not think it is peculiar, I will transcribe a few sentences from Dr. Channing; and this I do the more willingly because I hope these words, from that gifted man's pen, will lead you to a careful study of his valuable writings.

A BRIEF STATEMENT OF UNITARIANISM BY DR. CHANNING.

"Unitarianism amounts to this—That there is one God, even the Father, and that Jesus Christ is not that one God, but his son and messenger, who derived all his powers and glories from the Universal Parent, and who came into the world not to claim supreme homage for himself, but to carry up the soul to his Father as the only Divine Person, the only ultimate object of religious worship. To us this doctrine seems to have descended from the throne of God, and to invite and attract us thither. To us it seems to come from the Scriptures, with a voice loud as the sound of many waters, and as articulate and clear as if Jesus, in a bodily form, were pronouncing it in our ears. That we desire to propagate this doctrine we do not deny. It is a treasure which we wish not to confine to ourselves, which we dare not lock up in our own breasts. We regard it as given to us for others, as well as for ourselves. We should rejoice to spread it through this great city (New York), to carry it into every dwelling, and to send it far and wide to the remotest settlements of our country. We regard it as the highest, most important, most efficient truth, and therefore demanding a firm testimony, and earnest efforts to make it known. We hold, indeed, nothing to be essential to salvation but the simple and supreme dedication of the mind, heart, and life to God and to his will. This inward and practical devotedness to the Supreme Being, we are assured is attained, and accepted, under all the forms of Christianity. We believe, however, that it is favoured by that truth which we maintain as by no other system of faith. We regard Unitarianism as peculiarly the friend of inward, living, practical religion. For this we value it; for this we would spread it;

and we desire none to embrace it but such as shall seek and derive from it this celestial influence.

"We prize and would spread our views, because we believe that they reveal God to us in greater glory, and bring us nearer to him than any other. We are conscious of a deep want, which the creation cannot supply—the want of a perfect being, on whom the strength of our love may be centred, and of an Almighty Father, in whom our weaknesses, imperfections, and sorrows may find resource—and such a Being and Father Unitarian Christianity sets before us; for this we prize it above all price. We can part with every other good. We can endure the darkening of life's fairest prospects. But this bright consoling doctrine of one God, even the Father, is dearer than life, and we cannot let it go. Through this faith, everything grows brighter to our view. Born of such a Father, we esteem our existence an inestimable gift. We meet everywhere our Father, and his presence is as a sun shining on our path. We see him in his works, and hear his praise rising from every spot which we tread. We feel him near in our solitudes, and sometimes enjoy communion with him more tender than human friendships. We see him in our duties, and perform them more gladly, because they are the best tribute we can offer to our Heavenly Benefactor. Even the consciousness of sin, mournful as it is, does not subvert our peace; for, in the mercy of God, as manifest in Jesus Christ, we can see an inexhaustible fountain of strength, purity, and pardon for all who, in filial reliance, seek these heavenly gifts. Through this faith, we are conscious of a new benevolence springing up to our fellow-creatures, purer and more enlarged than natural affection. Towards all mankind, we see a rich and free love flowing from the Common Parent, and, touched by his love, we are the friends of all. We compassionate the most guilty, and would win them back to God. Through this faith, we receive the happiness of an ever enlarging hope. There is no good too vast for us to anticipate for the universe or for ourselves from such a Father as we believe in. We hope from him what we deem his greatest gift, even the gift of his own Spirit, and the happiness of advancing for ever in truth and virtue, in power and love, in union of mind with the Father and the Son."

Yours truly,

JOHN R. BEARD.

LETTER III.—REASONS WHY I AM A UNITARIAN.

I AM A UNITARIAN BECAUSE, 1ST, UNITARIANISM IS INTELLIGIBLE: 2ND, BECAUSE IT IS A REALITY; 3RD, BECAUSE IT IS REASONABLE.

MY DEAR EDWARD,—I am glad you have carefully perused my former communications. I thank you for the frank statement of the difficulties that the study of them has suggested to your mind. Yes; it is only the faintest outline that I sent you. What could you expect? "All your religion?" No; all our religion could not be compressed into a folio volume, much less a letter. The ethics of Unitarianism—Unitarianism in its multiform practicable developments and applications—can, in these communications, receive no more than a passing notice or two. Do not expect impossibilities. A few leading points will be touched on in what I shall further write to you. As, however, you seem to have formed but an imperfect notion of the import and bearing of what I have said, I shall put the same ideas in somewhat different phraseology, and in so doing briefly mark the relations in which Unitarianism stands to other forms of religion. You are so unused to any statements of religious doctrine, except what are called "evangelical," that it is no wonder you think my exposition somewhat scanty. Ere you have finished the reading of what is to come, you will, I am confident, acknowledge that the ideas which it contains are very prolific, and the system they form very rich. As little am I surprised that you find the notice I have taken of the Holy Spirit insufficient. With me the Holy Spirit is God in Christ and the Christian Church. Now, since God, as Jesus declares, is Spirit, and since God is holy, and since, also, God is ever moving in the hearts of holy men, to mention God is in some sense to designate the Holy Spirit, or Spirit of God, However, the specific Christian application of the term will not pass unnoticed. Only, do not expect a systematic treatise on divinity, when I undertake nothing more than a few popular sketches, designed to give you some general acquaintance with the views I hold and the ground on which I stand. I shall divide what I have to advance under a number of heads termed reasons. These it is which make me a Unitarian. Here I am held fast bound by necessity. Pressed upon by these considerations, I can do no other than be a Unitarian. And being a Unitarian, I should not think myself an honest man, much less a faithful disciple of the Great Apostle of truth, did I not avow my Unitarianism, and do what in me lies for its propagation. God be praised that you have resolved to give due heed to the great questions that are to pass in review.

First, then, a few words of further explanation. Unitarianism is that view of the Gospel which owns one God, the Father of all, who sent his Son to be the Saviour of the world, and gives his Spirit to inspire, guide, and comfort the true members of his Son's Church. Three objects are here presented to our reverent attention. 1st. The Father, who is the only living and true God, and as such the source of all the benefits of the Gospel. 2nd. The Son, who, as the Son, derives from the Father whatever he bestows on the world. And, 3rd. The Holy Spirit, or the Spirit of God—that is, God in and through Christ continuing and completing, in the various ministries of the Church, the gracious work "foreordained from the foundation of the world," carried forward in every land on the earth's surface by suitable ministrations, specially declared and promoted by Moses and the prophets, and fully showed forth and proclaimed in the life, teachings, death, and resurrection of Jesus of Nazareth. Considered in relation to the origin, design, tendency, and result of the Gospel, these three objects are one, for, from first to last, the Gospel is simply the gift of God's grace, designed for the salvation of the world. This unity of operation implicates a unity of source. That source is the one God, who communicates himself to the world through his Son and through his Spirit. Indeed, a fourfold operation is indicated in sacred Scripture, for God appears there (1) as the Creator and (2) as the Sanctifier of his intelligent creatures; and in order to be their Sanctifier, he pours forth on all reverent hearts, and specially on the followers of Christ, the blessed influences of (3) his Holy Spirit and concentrating all needful light, love, and power in (4) his Son, lifts him to his own right hand, and makes him the dispenser of spiritual life to the world. This view, which is the view given in the Bible, acknowledges the one God, the Father, of (*out of*) whom are all things, and one Lord Jesus Christ, by (*through*) whom are all things, and one Holy Spirit, who cleanses and hallows the children of God. The view, you will observe, is simply and exclusively religious. In other words, it deals with spiritual powers from first to last, Beginning with God the Creator, the primal and the eternal spiritual power, it sets him forth as working for the spiritual instruction and elevation of mankind by spiritual agencies. which spiritual agencies are the outpouring of his own divine Spirit, first in Christ, and then through Christ, on all who believe in Christ, that through Christ and Christ's Church he may communicate himself to the beings whom for that very purpose he made in his own image; and having accomplished the grand result, be all in all. Indeed, the Bible is the great repository of spiritual forces. In it religion is ever spirit and life, or spiritual life. The truth which it unfolds, the wisdom which it fosters, the salvation of which it is the record and one of the principal channels, are all great religious or spiritual powers and blessings. Of notions it knows nothing. Opinions it never enjoins. Speculation is wholly foreign to its spirit. With essences and modes of being it never deals. The phraseology of the schools and the decisions of the creeds are mere human additions to the Bible,—foreign accretions sprung from Greek arguing, and Latin systematizing, and monkish narrowness. They are human attempts to fathom the unfathomable, to define the undefinable, to map out the infinite. The grand religious generalities of the Bible they contract to the small dimensions of theological metaphysics, and harden them into the petrifications of human opinions. If Unitarianism did no more than offer a practical and living protest to a scholastical theology, it would do enough to justify its existence, and claim at least my respect. But while it says "No" to men's traditions, it says "Yes" to God's revelations, and the substance of those revelations is the one God, who made heaven and earth, and who governs and blesses his great human family by placing his Spirit in all who seek and love his truth, and by giving that Spirit, beyond all measure and comparison, to Christ, that through him he may feed all who hunger, refresh all who are thirsty, forgive the penitent, redeem the sinful, recall the wandering, and so reconcile all men to himself.

Such is Unitarianism. Such, at least, is a faint outline of the view of the spirit and tenor of the biblical religion as conveyed to my mind by a not superficial study of the sacred Scriptures. That view I denominate Unitarianism, because at its centre stands the unity of God—the one God of the Bible, the God of the patriarchs, the God of Moses, the God of the prophets, the God, and as the God, so the Father, of the Lord Jesus Christ.

Regarding these facts in respect to the religion of the world, we see that the Gospel is monotheism with a paternal Deity, in opposition to polytheism, and Unitarianism in opposition to Trinitarianism—that is, the acknowledgment of one God in one person, or one God, properly so called, in contrast with one God in three persons, or one God, improperly so called. Trinitarianism, indeed, pretends to be monotheistic; but it cannot be monotheistic without losing its own character, or incurring the danger of being tritheistic. As a matter of fact, it tends towards monotheism in cultivated minds and religious natures, and it tends towards tritheism in popular apprehension, and in popular forms of worship. Unitarianism, on the contrary, is, and can be, nothing else than monotheistic. It is, indeed, Christian monotheism, in all due severity, in contradistinction to Ecclesiastical tripersonalism, which ever borders on tritheism.

With these explanations, I proceed to assign some reasons why I am a Unitarian instead of a Trinitarian Christian.

1. *I am a Unitarian because Unitarianism is intelligible.* Unitarianism makes two statements—God is one; Christ is a human being, filled with God's spirit. First—God is one.

That is, God is one being, one mind, one spirit. This statement is intelligible. I learn what it means by looking within, for I myself am one being, one mind, one spirit. This one spirit who, as such, is intelligent, is also paternal. I know what a paternal spirit is, for I myself am a paternal spirit. Accordingly, my own inner sense is to me an image of God. I have no need to go for instruction to the schools. God, in revealing himself as one, and as a Father, bids me look on my own soul, and see there a miniature of himself. This is teaching alike easy and simple—so easy and so simple that it may be apprehended by babes in understanding; at the same time it is so deep and so sublime that it cannot be, as it never has been, surpassed by the highest thoughts of the best philosophy. Of Trinitarianism, on the contrary, no definition has ever been given which, if intelligible, did not savour of heresy or polytheism. God is three and one. One what?—One God. Three what?—Three Gods? But three Gods is polytheism, and unless three and one can be the same, must be discarded. Supposing, then, that it is indispensable to preserve the unity, wherein shall we place the trinity? Is it a triplicity? A threefold God is a phrase without meaning, simply because a threefold human mind does not exist. You say that it is a tripersonality. What do you mean by the term? A person is an individual intelligence, as Peter, James, and John. God, then, is one being in whom are three other beings, and so God is at once four beings, or four intelligences. This you will not allow; and if you did allow it, I could not apprehend it. You reply that *person* is taken in a peculiar sense. Tell me what the sense is which you attach to person? You cannot? Say person denotes character. Then God is one being with three characters. What the meaning of this statement may be in regard to God I know not, but such a statement in regard to a man would destroy the moral unity of him of whom it was asserted, and so bring him into disrepute. If you give preference to a term of darker import, and say that the persons are "somewhats," you must not be surprised if you are told, that you try to explain what is dark by what is darker. In these exigencies, a refuge has been sought in the term distinction—"God is one with three distinctions." The refuge gives no shelter, for it reduces the three persons to three distinctions, and so, making the Father a distinction, the Son a distinction, the Holy Ghost a distinction, undeifies the Deity, without presenting an intelligible idea. Indeed, to declare that a being is, in any sense, properly three and one, is to make a statement which conveys no meaning to my mind, because it takes that being out of the class of known existences, and makes him *sui generis*—that is, the sole of his kind. Of a being, however, who is sole of his kind no man can know anything. Such a being is an anomaly in the universe; an inexplicable enigma, of whom anything may be said, because nothing can be known. "Understandest thou what thou readest?" is a question which Philip put to the eunuch. Understandest thou what thou believest? is a question which may be put to the Trinitarian. And until he can put his belief in an intelligible shape, how can he comply with the apostolic injunction—"In understanding be men." In vain does he rejoin, "It is a mystery," for he cannot characterize any doctrine, the terms of which and the import of which are hidden from his eyes. Of a thing of which you are ignorant, all you can say is, "I do not know." But knowledge is the special privilege, and so the great characteristic, of the Christian. The Christian knows God, for he knows himself, the child of God, and he knows Christ, the image of God. That knowledge, which the Saviour himself described as involving eternal life, includes not the faintest outline of tripersonality. The mind of man is one —simply one: the mind of Christ is one—simply one. These are the Scriptural mirrors of the mind of God, and so God is one—simply one.

I said, also, that Christ is a human being (Luke iv. 22; John i. 45; vi. 42) filled with God's spirit (John iii. 34). Like the first, the second element in Unitarianism is intelligible. The reason is, that you and I are human beings, and being human beings, we know what is meant, when it is said, that Jesus was a human being. Here there is no cloud, no obscurity, no question. The moment, however, that you introduce speculative elements, you find yourself in mist, fog, or thick and palpable darkness. Jesus was a man, Trinitarianism declares, and yet denies that he was the Son of Joseph. If he was the son of Mary only, then he was born out of the ordinary manner, and so was a being *sui generis*, or a being standing by himself. In vain are we reminded that Adam had no human father. The cases are not parallel, for neither had he a human mother. Besides, Adam was the first of his race, and every first must come directly from God. When the type is once given by the Deity, the Deity uniformly confines himself to the type. But in Jesus the type is departed from, and wholly deserted. To him alone a human father is denied. He consequently stands alone, the only one who, being called a man, had no man for his father. Such a being is not a man, whatever he may be called, or all the grounds of our knowledge are uncertain and unreliable.

Speculation, denying Joseph to be the father of Jesus, goes further, and declares that Christ existed before he came into this world, not as all things and all beings existed, namely, in God's eternal thought and purpose, but in his own proper person. If so, then Christ was a pre-existent spirit, embodied in a human form. Who knows what that means? No one—the statement is unintelligible—words, mere words, words without the shadow of an idea, for of such a being we have neither, in our thought, nor in our experience, the faintest counterpart, or the most rudimentary germ.

Without pursuing speculation into its darker recesses, turn to the Scripture, where you find Christ described as having the spirit of God without measure. The corresponding truth is, that we have the spirit of God with measure (John iii. 34). Having the spirit of God ourselves, we can understand what is meant when it is said, that Christ had the spirit of God. The distinction, too, which the Bible makes between Christ and Christians is clear, for it is a matter of degree, great though the difference is (John xvii. 11). What we have in part, Christ has in the whole. Christ possessed all of God's spirit which God could give to a human being made perfect, and which a human being made perfect could receive. Christ, then, does not stand alone, is not a unique being, is not sundered from the race he came to save; but since he brings help to man, he shares their nature, and so sympathizes with their weaknesses, and bears their sorrows; yet, standing at their head, raises them, by the attraction of his own vital forces, upwards to himself (Heb. ii. 9,* *seq.;* vii. 26; John xii. 32). On our part, we are able to enter into the sufferings which a brother underwent on our behalf. We know what Christ suffered when he was hungry, when he was thirsty, when he wept, when he wrestled with temptation; when he was buffeted, mocked, and derided; when, in his last agony, he discerned, with his closing eyes, his bereft and

* For the correct translation of this passage, and many other mistranslations in the authorized version, see "A Revised English Bible, the Want of the Church;" by J. R. Beard. Simpkin, Marshall, and Co., London.

woe-stricken mother. All these griefs we can understand and appreciate, if Christ was truly and properly man; but make him God, make him a spirit descended from a higher sphere, detained here but a few years, and shortly about to return to his own home of everlasting peace and bliss, and you confound all my ideas; act strongly on my imagination you may, but in the same degree you bewilder my intelligence, and compel me to revive questions forced by speculation out of the simple hearts of primitive believers, as to whether Christ suffered in reality or in appearance, how the impassible God could have suffered at all, and how a celestial spirit, who, as celestial, must have been rich even on earth in holiest affections, sublimest thoughts, and brightest anticipations, could have suffered eclipse from the petty and transient clouds of earthly humiliation. Unworthy of divine or celestial love, is the supposition that it could have been darkened, much less quenched, by diabolical wiles, or sacerdotal rage, or even the deep shades of the valley of death.

2. *I am a Unitarian because Unitarianism is a reality.* The real is known from the unreal by its correspondence with the realities of our own being—the realities of our own experience. How do you distinguish a genuine coin from an adulterated one? By its look, its ring, its weight. You look at the sovereign, you ring it, you weigh it, and so ascertain that it is sterling gold. How do you distinguish true love from feigned love? By applying to it the test of your own sound affection, and by the test of experience. Here you have no difficulty. Did you ever mistake a false cry of pain, of joy, for a true one? The very sound of the voice betrays all counterfeit sentiments. In the same way you distinguish spiritual realities from spiritual unrealities. Take the Athanasian creed into your hands, read it, study it—is that a spiritual reality?

Does it correspond to anything in your own thought, your own spirit? You do not even know what it means. Then take it and try to live upon it—do you find in it the bread of life? You cannot even make it a part of your spiritual nature; no deeper than the memory will it go. It is a heap of the husks of human speculation, and not the manna which God gives from heaven to be the life of the world. On the contrary, Unitarianism is reality. Real is the idea of the one God; real is the idea of God the Father; real is the idea of Jesus of Nazareth, the son of Joseph and Mary; real is the idea of Christ the Son of God; real is the idea of God's spirit dwelling in all good men, and dwelling superabundantly in the great Head of human kind. The life of Christ, which in one sense, is a summary of the Gospel, as it is the substance of Unitarianism, is a grand cluster of spiritual realities. Real is his birth; real his domestic training; real his communion with God; real his preparation for his public work, and his call to that work; real the temptation he underwent when on the point of entering thereon; real the hardships he endured; real his hunger, his thirst, his weariness; real that agony in the garden; real those throes of the cross. So, too, real was his celestial light, and real his divine power; real every word he spake as taught of God, and real every deed he did in putting forth the divine power that was in him. Equally real is the influence he now exercises in the souls and the lives of the faithful, real the blessings he bestows, real the transformations he effects, real the joy he inspires, and real the immortal life he gives. All these things are real; we know them to be real; they are as real as our daily food, as our purest affections, as our nobler life. Indeed, they are the reality of realities—the life-blood, the strength, the vigour, the happiness of our souls. Pre-eminently is Unitarianism a religion of reality.

So far as it is true to itself, it is as real as God, as real as Christ, as real as human life, as real as moral power, as real as home, as real as a father's example and a mother's love. Knowingly and consciously it takes to itself nothing but what is real; and the unreal, or that of which it doubts the reality, it leaves on one side, assured that only what is real can be of God, who, in the highest sense, is the Great Reality.

How dissimilar—to give one instance—the doctrine of the two natures in Christ. From Christ that doctrine takes all reality, leaving him neither God nor man. What reality can you recognize in a being who, though finite, is yet infinite? who, though limited to a point on the earth's surface, yet fills the universe; who is partially ignorant, yet fully wise; who is and is not absolutely good; who cannot die, yet dies; who is at once hungry and full; who thirsts, but is not thirsty; who weeps, while possessed of "joy unspeakable and full of glory?" Stripping Christ of all reality, the doctrine robs him of all power, at least over human hearts, and were it really believed and acted on, would make the living Son of the living God once more a corpse, and consign him to a sepulchre more hard to burst open than that of Joseph of Arimathea.

3. *I am a Unitarian because Unitarianism is reasonable.* By this statement I do not mean that Unitarianism merely conforms to the rules of logical thought; still less that it recognizes in reasoning the organ of religious discovery; still less again, that it makes its light the measure of divine truth. What I mean is, that the truth of which it consists is in harmony with the great laws and tendencies of human life. If God made man in his own image, then man's image must more or less correspond to the divine mind. If Christ is emphatically the image of God, then Christ is the portrait of the supreme reason. It follows that all that comes from God

is an outflow of reason, that is of truth. As such, it is as germane and suitable to man's mind as the sunshine, the rain, the air, and the dew to the grain, the shoot, the ear, the flower, the fruit. Hence, to be reasonable is to be divine. And hence Christ is divine, because reason perfected in a man. Christianity, therefore, is reason, and in one sense reason is Christianity. And hence, too, every human mind is Christian in proportion as it is reasonable. The unreasonable is unchristian. That which contradicts reason contradicts Christianity. If God is one, one also is God's plan of action. If the Gospel is from God, the Gospel is divine reason made easy for man. To suppose that divine truth can set reason at nought, is to suppose that God traverses his own paths and contradicts his own purposes. It is true that I may take that for unreason, which is the highest reason. But then the lesson to give me is not to prostrate my intelligence, but to clear my sight and elevate my point of view. It is the pure in heart that see God. Equally certain is it that many see only the cloud, without discerning the light that shines at its back. Bid me wait, and meanwhile worship and serve, but do not threaten me with woe because I declare that to be dark which is dark to me. The very fact that Christ came supposes that I need aid. But equally does it suppose that I am able to receive aid; and if I am able to receive aid, I am able to know what aid is. It is into a genial bosom that the soil receives the seed, and so the seed germinates and grows. Between the seed and the soil there is a pre-established harmony. A similar harmony exists between truth and the human mind. Intended the one for the other, the two bear a divine correspondence and suitability. The correspondence lies in the essence of the two. The recognition of that correspondence on our part is spontaneous and inevitable.

The suitability is felt and acknowledged the moment the two come into vital contact. Here, as everywhere in God's world, like seeks and owns its like. As is light to the eye, so is truth to the mind. As is the ear to sound, so is the soul to reason. Accordingly, the unreasonable is darkness, is discord. Indeed, unreasonableness is a nonentity relatively to God. It comes not from him; it tends not to him; it works not his work. Like darkness, it is a privation; like discord, it is a contrariety. And privation and contrariety are weakness and death in the soul.

Oh! wonderful is it that it should still be necessary to declare that the Gospel is one with man's deepest instincts, purest affections, highest thoughts, and noblest aims; and painful is it to feel it necessary to add, that whatever runs contrary to these divine currents in our souls is not from above, but from below. The necessity arises from the fact, that professors of the Gospel still throw the shield of divine authority before the dark and confused images of their own troubled fancies and diseased speculations. Is Unitarianism free from this error? By no means do I assert that my view or your view of truth contains nothing contrary to truth, or that any man's truth contains all God's truth. But this I may declare, that, as a general principle, Unitarianism recognizes the laws of reason as the laws of God. This recognition pervades Unitarianism. Religion itself is only the highest reason. Truth in reason is truth in religion. He that is nearest to reason is nearest to God, and so has the best and purest religion. Surely, in any issue, reason is perferable to unreason. If so, why not in religion? Religion is a universal power, and should be a universal presence in man's soul. But if the leaven is to leaven the whole lump, the leaven must conform to the nature and laws of the lump. Never would our food give strength and joy were it not, in its nature, capable of entering into combination with every particle of our frame. When Jesus termed himself the "bread of life," he declared that the truth he brought from God was made for the human soul. Unitarianism takes Jesus at his word, and owns as divine manna that which looks like a gift from the heavenly Father, and tastes sweet and wholesome, like all other divine nutriment. Other fruits grown in Paradise there may be, for which, at present, we have no relish, but, if such there are, they will in some way declare, in time, their celestial origin, and so bring their welcome with them.

Meanwhile, the certain is preferable to the uncertain, and our loyalty to God forbids us to own anything but what bears God's image and inscription. It is but in part that we know God's illimitable truth. But this we know, that where our ignorance begins our tongue must be silent, and that to strain belief is only to make our words untrue and our minds unnatural and unsound. It is, indeed, often a duty to trust where we cannot trace, and worship God in the darkness of the holy of holies; but we dare not call darkness light; nor dare we own as divine that which wears the impress of the human. And so often has what men call mystery been made to veil, and so to recommend absurdity, that we think it our duty to be on our guard when required to accept a doctrine though, or because, it is mysterious. Certainly, in the Scripture, the Gospel is offered as light, God is described as "light, and in him is no darkness at all," while of Christ it is said, "In him was light, and the light was the life of the world" (John i. 4). May that light and that life become yours. Such, my dear Edward, is the earnest prayer of

Yours truly,

JOHN R. BEARD.

LETTER IV.—REASONS WHY I AM A UNITARIAN.

(Continued.)

I AM A UNITARIAN BECAUSE, 4TH, UNITARIANISM IS TRUE; 5TH, POSITIVE, PERMANENT, AND UNIVERSAL; 6TH, FAVOURABLE TO FREEDOM; 7TH, PROGRESSIVE; 8TH, SCRIPTURAL.

4. *I am a Unitarian because Unitarianism is true.* All reality is truth. The fact is consecrated in one of the underlying thoughts of the Biblical religion. The Biblical name for truth and reality is the same word. The Bible identifies truth and reality. With a regard to fact, which would be the highest philosophy were it not the simplest, yet deepest religious insight, the Bible making reality and truth the same, makes them both firm, stable, certain, and trustworthy. The word *Amen* is, in its root, the Biblical word for truth, reality, steadfastness, and reliability; and so the Bible itself is the great *Amen* to the religious yearnings of the human heart. God's truth in man's soul is a foundation of eternal adamant. God's religion is no mere matter of opinion. Opinion is a Latin word, and so of mere human origin, and has nothing to do with true religion. True religion, having God for its source, and man's soul for its earthly abode, is like the everlasting hills for stability and grandeur, and can no more totter or sink than the sun can fall or become extinct. And so faith in God's religion is "the anchor of the soul, sure and steadfast," cast within the harbour of God's own eternal repose. He that is one with the Christ of God, is one with the life which has neither beginning nor end, is one with the love which is the essence of God, is one with the truth which is God himself; for God is truth absolute, since he is the Father of lights, with whom there is no variableness, neither shadow of turning (James i. 17).

It is true, and can never be anything else but true, that "there is one God, and there is none other but he;" that the one God is the Father of all men, and specially the Father of Christ; that Jesus lived at Nazareth and died on Calvary; that he taught the truth that he had heard from God; that the truth he taught is the life of the world, and that every heart that has the sources of its life in Christ, becomes like Christ, "holy, harmless, and undefiled," and so is strong for every godlike work, and rich in spiritual peace and joy. These things are true. They are true because they are God's realities. They are known to be true to all to whom they are practically known—known to be true as certainly and as fully as our instinctive impulses are known to be true, as our highest law is known to be true, as moral obligations are known to be true. The man who lives as Christ lived, knows that he lives the true life of a man, as assuredly as he knows that the love of home is true love, and a life of benevolence the true life. Truth is only the correspondence of man's thought and man's act with God's realities, so that a human life, full of God's realities, is a simple utterance of God's truth. Indeed, the service of the one only God in his Son Jesus Christ, is the practical possession of the truth. And what is this but Unitarianism? In idea, at least, Unitarianism is a human embodiment of the spirit of the God and Father of the Lord Jesus Christ, and so is *the* truth. We have only to be what Unitarianism would make us, in order to know the truth by unmistakable signs and tokens, and in the knowledge to become wise, holy, and blessed.

5. *I am a Unitarian because Unitarianism is positive, permanent, and universal.* Unitarianism has indeed a negative side. A negative side is an indispensable element in all true religion. Truth must protest against error. Holiness must

protest against sin. Light must expel darkness. Abraham's migration was a protest. Moses came laden with a protest. The burthen of each of the prophets was almost all protest. Jesus, the last of the series, uttered the strongest and loudest protest. Like Unitarianism, his was a reformatory work. He laboured to carry the mind of his nation back to the grand thought of the one God, revealed in the opening words of Genesis, and expanded and made practical in the Decalogue. In his spirit all his true apostles have laboured, from Paul down to Luther, and from Luther down to Priestley and Channing. To protest against error is an essential element in all progressive endeavours. You cannot get men right unless you show them where they are wrong. The mere enunciation of general principles is only shooting arrows into the air. You must weed and drain your field before you sow your crop. This is the first duty of Unitarianism—a duty as yet performed only on a narrow stage. If not more emphatic, certainly more general and in a more noticeable form, must it, like Protestantism, say "No!" to all the falsities which have invaded the kingdom of God and usurped his throne in the heart of od's subjects. But Unitarianism denies only to affirm. As did Christ, it cleanses the temple, but leaves the temple itself standing, and standing in its own primitive grandeur and stability. Trinitarianism divested of its characteristics, becomes the Gospel. The unclothing now rapidly proceeding, is every day bringing the system nearer to the simple beauty of God's own truth. But then the change denotes the human origin of the opinions in which its distinctiveness consists. Whereas, Unitarianism is now what it ever was, and what it ever will and must be. Fundamentally the same is the truth of one God the Father, and one Lord Jesus Christ, now as when it was proclaimed by the

Apostles and by their Master himself. "As it was in the beginning, is now, and ever shall be, world without end," though forming part of the Trinitarian liturgy, is true only of the simple elements of the Unitarian faith.

An ancient father of the Church proposed Catholicity as the test and measure of Christian truth. "That is true," said he, and his voice prevailed, "that is true which has been believed always, everywhere, and by all." I accept the rule, and ask, what form of orthodoxy can endure its application? Every part of orthodoxy is a variable quantity. Not one doctrine is there but has grown, flourished, and decayed. Not one doctrine is there which, if owned by me, has not been disowned by you. It is only of the ultimate and simplest form of Christianity that the epithet Catholic can be truly employed. Unitarianism alone possesses the attribute of universality. From the days of Christ down to the days of Luther, and from the days of Luther down to the present hour, all, at all times, and in all places, have owned one God, the Father, and one Lord Jesus Christ, nor will the day ever come when any disciple will cease to make that confession. Add to the confession men may, but in adding to it they only signify their credence and attest its Catholicity.

6. *I am a Unitarian because Unitarianism is favourable to freedom.* "Where the Spirit of the Lord is there is liberty." Liberty is the first attribute of religion as existing in the human soul. Without freedom, religion has no life. As you must breathe before you can live, so you must be free before you can be religious. What is religion but the free act of the will of man adopting as its own the will of God? What is religion but the free act of the soul bathing itself in the ocean of the divine life? The mind must be free if its movements

are to be natural. The mind must be free if its acceptance of divine truth is to be real and efficacious. A manacled hand cannot work with due effect. A bandaged leg can do no better than limp. A body in chains is powerless. God made the mind free, and free must the mind remain if it is to do God's work and answer God's purposes. But is that mind free which is burdened with lengthy creeds and cumbrous catechisms? Is that mind free whose conclusions are prescribed beforehand? Is that mind free on which Trinitarianism is enforced by the threat of eternal perdition? To talk of freedom in such cases is a mockery. The high priests, when they had nailed Christ to the cross, bade him come down that they might believe. What else do you do, if you say I am free to inquire, but can be safe only if I end by agreeing with yourself? Scarcely less are you to blame if, to protect your own opinions, you raise against me a hue-and-cry. Popular clamour is guilty of the death of Christ. Those who wage war against free thinkers, with prejudice as a chief weapon of offence, have no claim to the honourable title of friends of religious liberty. Yet are not these the arms with which an attempt has been made to hunt Unitarianism down? The noble stag still stands at bay, and so stands because its limbs are all free, and they are all free because they have been duly exercised in God's air and God's sunshine, and on the green hills of God's nutritious truths. Yes, Unitarianism *is* free. As far as anything human can be perfect, Unitarianism is perfectly free. It is free to think, to inquire, to learn, to speak, to act. It is free to be and remain what it is. It is free to go whithersoever it is called of God. It is free to use all its faculties, to cultivate all its capabilities, to seek truth in every part of God's universe, and to receive into its substance all the light which God may offer. In consequence, it makes free men, and free men are ever strong men, and strong men cannot fail to do some work for God.

7. *I am a Unitarian because Unitarianism is progressive.* Liberty is a guarantee of progress. Without progress there is no life. The religious life is in its nature progressive. Growth is as essential to the Christian as it is to the plant. The highest natures grow most; and true religion is, of all powers, most favourable to growth. This growth is true growth. It is growth in God's own realities. Even in his knowledge of God and Christ does the Christian grow. The idea of both becomes to him grander, brighter, deeper, more impressive. But the idea itself he never abandons. The one Father and the one Brother are constant quantities, however they may open out and shine forth in his soul. Such expansions the Christian earnestly desires. They are the appropriate rewards of loving service. Illimitable, too, are they, for their developments and applications partake of their own infinitude. Wherever they go, the true disciple is not only prepared but delighted to follow. Knowing that God's truth is inexhaustible, he looks for constantly new disclosures; and, when they come, he welcomes them as God's most precious gifts. Such is the spirit of Unitarianism. In its essence it is progressive. It acknowledges that "the man of God" cannot and dare not stand still. It sets limits neither to inquiry nor to the results of inquiry. Content to leave itself in the hands of God, it asks only for truth. Goethe passed from earth with the words, "Light! more light!" on his lips. The same is the request made to his Heavenly Father by the Unitarian, whether living or dying.

8. *I am a Unitarian because Unitarianism is Scriptural.* The fact is involved in much of what I have previously advanced. The fact cannot be denied even by Trinitarians. The doctrine of one God, the Father, and one Lord Jesus

Christ, is admitted by all Christians as scriptural and true, as far as they go. Additions are indeed made, but their value may be estimated by the fact, that they are as various as the generations of men, the climates of the earth; as various as the philosophies, the Churches, almost the individuals from whom they come, and whose image they bear. However, they unite to declare the essence of Unitarianism scriptural. "Insufficient," not "false," is what they say of it. They thus concede the scripturality of our fundamental doctrines. Whatever else a disciple of Christ may be, he must be a Unitarian. Declare, if you will, that Unitarianism is only milk for babes, still by your own statement, it is milk. Who will deny that the Scripture proclaims one God the Father, and one Lord Jesus Christ? Who hesitates to make these scriptural verities articles of his faith? Who will assert that they are not at the centre of his religious life? Is it not made a reproach to Unitarianism that its assumed distinction of God's oneness is no distinction at all? Does not the Trinitarian assert that he too is a Unitarian? Is it not maintained that the unity of God is the common property of Christendom? If so, then, by the doctrine of Trinitarians, it is only in its negatives that Unitarianism is wrong. The denial of the Trinity—the denial of the Trinity of the authorised statements of the notion, that is, the denial of the Trinity of the creeds, especially of the Athanasian creed—the creed sanctioned alike by age and numbers—that makes the distinction between a Trinitarian and a Unitarian. Consequently, every one is a Unitarian who stands on this side the dividing line: and, verily, Unitarian in spirit and tendency are all who renounce the established formularies. What a proof of the direction in which the visible Church is going, for out of the Catholic pale, believers in the pseudo-Athanasian form are very few!

Doubtless, the Protestant Churches of England are fast Unitarianising. The fact is a tacit confession of the Unitarian character of the Bible—of all Unitarian manuals the best. And in the issue which still remains as between attenuated forms of the Trinity and the simple and stable truth of One God the Father, and one Lord Jesus Christ, the sole point is, are Trinitarians justified in their additions? This they have to show. It is their duty to adduce the proofs; our duty limits itself to the examination of the evidence. The evidence has been weighed in the balance and found wanting. Not by Unitarians only have your proof-texts been judged insufficient. Insufficient have they been pronounced by yourselves. Not one text is there, from the beginning of Genesis to the end of the Apocalypse, but has been abandoned by some Trinitarian critic. One after the other, every fort and every citadel has been surrendered. The argument stands thus:—You admit our position and surrender your own; you acknowledge the unity and confess the unscripturality of the Trinity. Accordingly, the more thoughtful and fair-minded of those who write on the Trinitarian side have now taken their stand on interpretations of the doctrine which hardly differ from Unitarianism, or which are so obscure as to convey little, if any, meaning.

Without a question, monotheism is the doctrine of the Bible. Without a question, Christianity stands at the head of monotheistic religion. The Bible makes it equally clear that there is a strong tendency in less cultivated minds to fall away from monotheism, more or less. Not less clear is it that God, in his care of the Hebrew Church, wrought in every possible way to withstand that tendency. It is not too much to say that monotheism is dear to God. No wonder, for the slightest departure from monotheism is departure from God. And what is departure from God, but the first step to either polytheism or pantheism. If you will not have the God of the Bible for your God, you run the risk of denying God altogether, or of confounding the Creator with the works of his hands. A danger so imminent, yet so fearful, should make every one anxious to cleave to biblical simplicity. And the existence of the danger creates a strong presumption against any modified form of monotheism in the Christian Church. A similar presumption arises against the scripturality of any such modification. If God took such pains first to lead Israel to the acknowledgment of his sole Deity, and afterwards to keep him faithful to the grand truth, it is not easy to believe that he gave any authority by which his essential oneness might be qualified by any threeness whatever. Nor can it be pretended that a qualification of the kind is expressly taught in the New Testament.

At the best, Trinitarianism is but an inference, and no inference can be properly entitled a revelation. Indeed, the untenableness of the inference has been admitted, nay, avowed, and loudly declared, by Trinitarians no less learned than pious, who, failing to discover the Trinity in the Bible, have looked for its origin and its support in the Church. But if the Bible is not Trinitarian, then is it Unitarian. What else, indeed, can it be, when Jesus expressly declares his Father to be the only true God (John xvii. 3); and when, at the moment that he was about to enter into eternal life, he said, "I ascend to my Father and your Father, to my God and your God" (John xx. 17). So, then, Christ had a God, that God was his Father; the God and Father of Christ was the God and Father of his disciples. Equally was He the only true God. If the God and Father of Christ was the God and Father of Christ's disciples, then must He not be so for ever, and ought He not to be your God and Father? As Jesus declared his Father to be his God, so I avouch him to be my God, and as his Father was the only true God to Jesus, so the only true God shall He be to me. Accordingly, I am a Unitarian because Unitarianism is scriptural.

When you have carefully considered these things, you shall again hear from

Yours truly,

John R. Beard.

LETTER V.—REASONS WHY I AM A UNITARIAN.

(*Continued.*)

I AM A UNITARIAN BECAUSE UNITARIANISM IS—9TH, SALUTARY; 10TH, PRACTICAL; 11TH, CONDUCIVE TO PIETY; 12TH, HONOURABLE TO THE SAVIOUR.

My Dear Edward,—9. *I am a Unitarian because Unitarianism is salutary.* Salutary it must be if, as I have shown, it is intelligible, real, true, liberal, and scriptural. Intelligible ideas are ideas which, corresponding to the nature, laws, and wants of the mind, the mind can appropriate and convert into its own substance, and so live thereon, as the hart on the green pastures of the river-side. Spiritual realities are the staff of man's spiritual life. Truth is the "feast of fat things" which God has provided for those who love him. Liberty is to our higher life what the breezes, and the sun-light, and movement are to the cedars of Lebanon.

Scriptural knowledge is the sap of the soul. And so all who have eaten the bread which God's own hand supplies know that it is salutary as it is sweet. That bread, divine in its origin, is, on that account, adapted to the wants of our

counter, and is the bosom companion of the merchant on the exchange. In the nursery it fills and moves the mother's heart, while it visits the prisoner in his cell, and consoles the captive in his dungeon. This I mean is the spirit, the aim, the tendency of Unitarianism. Nothing that is human does it consider excluded from the circle of its concern. Religion with it is, like its source, all pervading. It is religious to teach the ignorant child to read, no less than to redeem the slaves of sense and sin. Most salutary must such a religion be. Most salutary Unitarianism is wherever it is allowed to exercise its proper influence and produce its natural effects.

If Unitarianism is salutary, it is so far at least Christian, for Christ came to bring salvation. Salvation in the scriptural sense sums up the blessings of the Gospel in one word. But what is salvation? In the orthodox churches salvation is often escape from hell, escape from the wrath of God, escape from punishment. In reality, salvation is not a negative, but a positive good. Regarded commonly as a negative good, it is regarded also as an arbitrary gift—something put into a man, instead of something brought out of a man; something bestowed by God, not wrought out under God; something, in consequence, superinduced on the individual, therefore, something supernatural; as such, also, something mysterious, something standing apart from the inner man, and so compatible with evil dispositions, bad temper, unkindness at home, and sharp dealing abroad. The radical vices of the popular system are mainly two—first, it makes too little of human agency; second, it makes that agency to consist in the reception of a creed. If you accept evangelical orthodoxy, you are saved; if you refuse it, you are damned. All other considerations are sunk in this alternative. The opinion of a priest, a sect, a petty church, opens or closes the gates of heaven. On your assent to your neighbour's doctrine depends your eternal condition. What is this but papal infallibility in a Protestant shape? What is this but a supercession of the Scripture, and a usurpation of the judicial functions of the Omniscient? It is, moreover, a gross perversion of Scriptural truth. The faith which the Scripture requires is not assent, but trust; no mere act of the intellect, but a state, a movement of the heart. In a word, it is that confidingness in God and Christ which makes them its all. Faith, in consequence, is natural, deeply and strongly natural. It is the yearning of the heart toward God. It is the prayer of the heart for God's presence. It is a struggling toward the light. It is the outstretched hand of the drowning man. It is, "Lord, save or I perish." For at its root is a deep, vivid, and painful sense of want—a want like that of the hungry and thirsty when they are near fainting on the desert. This is the Scriptural faith. While it is spiritual need and spiritual desire on our part, it is, in regard to God, a simple acknowledgment of his all-sufficiency. Of the debates and decisions of the schools it knows nothing. All it knows is, that the fountain of life is there—fresh, full, overflowing—that is all it knows, and in that knowledge it is led to obtain all it wants,

Christian salvation, you thus see, is a spiritual good—a blessing suited to man's nature, and salutary to man's nature. It is, moreover, a good which impregnates the whole man, and so transforms and ennobles him. Of that great and most blessed change faith is the sap, and faith is active sympathy with Christ. By that sympathy we are ingrafted into the ever living vine, and receiving into our spirits its generous and enriching juices, live the divine life, and produce enduring fruit.

Most salutary must the Gospel be, for its object is to transfuse the life of Christ into the life of every individual man.

Christian salvation, in its full and proper sense, is a character moulded after the image of Christ.

It is the teaching of the fourth Gospel, that the intelligence which made the world was given to Christ. Here, too, Christ stands in the line, as well as at the head, of human kind. Reason is a part of our great human heritage. God's light shines in man's soul. In the soul of ordinary men the light is small and dim. In the soul of Christ the light was fullest and most brilliant. On that account Christ is *the* Son of God, while we are each only *a* son. But his supremacy is designed for our elevation. God in Christ illumines and saves the human race. Thus Christ is the light of the world. But spiritual light is spiritual power. The sun quickens, renews, and beautifies, as well as illumines. In consequence, the Gospel is "the power of God unto salvation," and "Christ is our righteousness, sanctification, and redemption." This he is not by imputation, but by God's grace and our own act. The latter is as necessary as the former. Even God cannot give unless man is willing to receive. It is ours to appropriate the spiritual food which God supplies; nor can we incorporate that food with our spirits unless we first gain an appetite from work, and by work set in movement all the vital activities of our souls. Christ, then, is God's own appointed channel of communication with his human children. As God, through the material sun, sends down choice blessings on man, so, through the Sun of Righteousness, does God give his own blessed Spirit to all who love and desire to serve him. Hence religion is a series of divine benefactions, and worship a stream of sunlike gratitude, and obedience an outflow of filial love. Hence, too, virtue is the ripened harvest of the soul—the rich crop of full-grown wheat; the total product and outcome of human life, enriched through Christ with the life of God.

Considered, too, as God's intelligence in a human being, Christ is, relatively to us, absolute spiritual truth and perfection. If so, the Gospel is God's word to man—the highest word God has yet spoken—the highest word man is capable of receiving. Of any possible manifestation of God in other ages and in other worlds we know nothing, and so should say nothing. Enough that Christ is all we want, and far more than we can as yet accept. The nearer now we get to Christ, the less shall we be disposed to speculaté, and the more shall we be content to worship in that true lowliness of mind which lifts the soul to God, and which Christ made the sole condition, as of his own favour, so of God's infinite grace. This oneness of Christ with God's supreme intelligence makes his Church into the great spiritual community, every member of which shares the blessed life of reverent, thankful, and obedient love. Thus God in Christ gives his own spirit to his children, and moulds them into his own likeness. The divine life interpenetrates the life of man, bestowing on the life of man somewhat of its own power and majesty. Christian salvation, then, is not a name, nor a form, but a reality. It is no theological theorem, nor any legal scheme, nor any arbitrary device, but the transfusion of God's own goodness into the human soul. Hence Christian salvation is a new creation Therein God finishes and consummates the good work he began when he breathed into man the breath of life. Consequently, human life, from its first issue to its return to its source, is simply a stream of God's love and power. The world's history is one great theatre of God's action, and one grand display of God's perfect will.

You will not, my dear Edward, deny that the views here presented are salutary. I think you will acknowledge them to be also desirable. Not less surely are they intelligible. I cannot but hope they will prove acceptable to you. But then, observe, they proceed from me, and I am a Unitarian. The fact would be, with many, a discommendation—are you superior to the silly prejudice? Any way I am a Unitarian, because Unitarianism is salutary.

10. *I am a Unitarian because Unitarianism is practical.* Of all great personages, who so practical as Jesus Christ? "He went about doing good," is the whole of his history in one brief sentence. Like God's, his beneficence was a continual efflux. As the sun rises on the seventh day no less than the first, so Jesus spared not to do good on the Sabbath-day. What more practical than the spirit of that fine declaration, "the Sabbath was made for man, and not man for the Sabbath." Jesus is the great utilitarian. Only use with him always meant the highest use. In this mould has the spirit of Unitarianism been cast. With us, all outer things are of value as they minister to the inner man. With us, all outer things minister to the inner man, if imbued with a religious spirit. In the true kingdom of God the lowliest service is divine service. The door-keeper who owns and feels the presence of God in his temple, is nearer God than the high-priest who offer none but a material sacrifice. A pure heart makes the hands pure. A noble self-sacrifice ennobles the humblest office. Religion is not a form—not a ritual, not a creed, but a spirit and a power working within and shining without. In consequence, religion may live and breathe in the kitchen, the nursery, the counting-house, the senate. Hence is it that Unitarians take part in all great social movements, exercising an influence far greater than their numbers, position, or wealth. Hence, too, is it that they pay special regard to education, not only in their own families, but in mechanics' and other popular institutions. Hence, also, their well-known attachment to civil as well as religious liberty. Nor can it be

denied that the practical character of their religion conduces no little to their success in trade and commerce. The Unitarian mind is pre-eminently practical. Here lies its danger as well as its worth. Disregarding the form that it may get to the substance, it may miss the substance without retaining the form. Yet, in general, the substance is secured. Unitarianism loves the activities and struggles of the living, breathing world. It loves the air and the sunshine, the breeze and the upland. It shrinks not from the mountain steep, nor stops till it has reached its goal. Hence a brave as well as robust spirit. Hence, vigour, progress, success. How different the intellect that is "cabined, cribbed, and confined" by a narrow creed; that finds religion chiefly in the bended knee, the serious countenance, and the mortified heart; that, fearing to go wrong, can hardly go right; that, dreading heresy, misses the portal to truth, and intent mainly on avoiding the way of death, has no energy left for walking in the path of life.

11. *I am a Unitarian because Unitarianism is conducive to piety.* What I have just said will show you that by piety I do not mean monkish asceticism. True Christian piety is a manly virtue. He who was called the Son of Man, because he united in his life all manly excellencies, was pious as it becomes you and me to be pious. The piety of Jesus has two chief characters—it was devout, it was obedient Devout obedience sums up the sublime life of Christ. He worshipped and he obeyed his Father. Worship and work constitute true piety. If Christ is our example, we must combine worship with work. By worship we must prepare for work, and in work we must prepare for worship.

It cannot be denied that to adore and to obey, make up the whole course of Christ's public life. Did you ever reflect on these facts? Did you ever ask yourself what they say regarding the position of Christ in the scale of being? Did you ever see how beautifully they illustrate the sonship of Christ? Surely that is not Almighty God that is prostrate in prayer there on that Palestinian hill. Surely those groans that come from the garden of Gethsemane are not the voice of God. In truth they are a son's entreaties to a father. The face of Christ is towards the Infinite One. His lips move, his heart heaves, and the Father of all sends down his spirit to commune with the Son of his love. Truly filial the act; truly paternal the gift. The very word piety denotes the tender respect of a son towards a father. Herein is Jesus super-eminently great. Never son worshipped as he worshipped, and, therefore, never did a son obey as he obeyed. His obedience was the natural fruit of his worship. How entire, how unreserved, how unconditional that obedience. The reason is, that that obedience was piety in act, as that worship was piety in emotion.

You will observe, that this perfect piety springs wholly from the relation that subsisted between God and Christ. The relation was, on God's side paternal, on Christ's side filial. Perfect piety, then, is the piety which arises when the fatherhood of God and the sonship of man is fully realised. Where, then, among Christ's disciples, may we expect to find most true piety? Where, except in the Church whose distinctive quality is the recognition of the one God, even the Father, and the one Son, even Jesus, the son of Joseph and Mary? Depart from this Scriptural simplicity, and you at once find yourself in a tangled wood, where darkness and perplexity baffle your attempts to see, and disturbing your heart, make its movements unnatural and painful. What! God worship God! The man in Christ worship the God in

Christ! When Christ obeyed God, he obeyed himself! His submission to his Father's will was really submission to his own! that is—no submission at all! And so Christ had no higher law to obey! no infinite perfection to arise to! He was in himself the all in all—and yet he worshipped and obeyed! and yet, he said—"Not my will but thine be done!" Has Brahminism any contradictions more palpable and absurd?

But now, pass from these fond delusions, and ask yourself what can be so conducive to piety as faith in an Omnipotent Father. Does not that one word Father say everything? Is it not an assurance to us each of wisdom, love, authority on the part of God? and consideration, compassion, tenderness, long-suffering as well? On the part of man, what so fitting to call forth gratitude, love, reverence, trust? And are not these the very elements of which religious obedience is made? If faith in the Father of Jesus does not create in men work as well as worship, and so produce true piety, true piety is an impossibility. As a Unitarian, I know that I ought to be pre-eminently pious, and it is because I wish to attain so great a blessing that I cleave to my Unitarianism. Of shortcomings I am vividly conscious, but I am assured that the worst step I could take, in order to fill up the measure of my duty, would be to pass into a circle of religious influences far inferior to the one in which I am.

12. *I am a Unitarian because Unitarianism is honourable to the Saviour.* The influence on the Church of the feudalism of the middle ages, identified honour with position. Who so honourable as the king in the state, and the Pope in the church? Accordingly, to honour Christ was to place him on the throne of his Father. Now, it is beginning to be acknowledged that true honour consists in noble service. He is the

most honourable being who does most good with least self-consideration. Herein lies the honour even of God, who, without any self-regardingness, pours forth the full and constant streams of his love. Under God, whose goodness so ample as that of Christ, and whose goodness so disinterested? Christ, indeed, has an honour all peculiar to himself, for, though rich in the benignities and powers of his own soul, He renounced all that he might live a life of poverty for the good of man (2 Cor. viii. 9; comp. vi. 10). Possessed of the unqualified freedom of a mind which lives in God, he submitted to the lot of a slave that he might redeem men from slavery and death (Philip. ii. 6). And in that godlike work, what sympathies, and as what sympathies, so what sufferings, were his!

It is only the very good that can feel the terribleness of the very bad. It is only a soul strung to the harmonics of heaven that duly feels the jar and discord of the passions of earth. The pure and intense love of Christ made him keenly alive to the hatreds and strifes of men. Accordingly, the Scripture describes the Saviour as bearing our woes (Matt. viii. 17; comp. Rom. xv. 1; Gal. vi. 2). The statement does not mean merely that he bore them away, though doubtless bear them away he did. But he effected that most desirable end by enduring the pains which we endure. Such was his rich, deep, and intensely strung sympathy that his soul vibrated to every pang felt by those who were around him. Though young, you, my friend, are not a stranger to this noble fellow-feeling. As you have rejoiced with your mother in her joy, so you have wept with her in her grief. But the great and exquisitely tender heart of Christ shared in all our human sorrows with a poignancy and a depth of which you and I have but the faintest notion. Witness his groans and tears at the grave of Lazarus. "They were undue," declares the unbeliever. Alas! that common-place men will make themselves the standard of human kind. Sadder still, to know that they will own no greatness that stands above their pigmy height. In the rich and delicate sensibilities of his moral nature, Jesus has prevailing claims on our love, but that love arises into the most honouring reverence when he is seen consecrating all to the service of his kind. Benevolence so pure and generous is not only peerless, but very precious and very potent. The balm of such sympathy heals and cherishes, restores and strengthens, giving a fresh energy, and calling forth ardent gratitude. What honour greater than that of him who so forgets himself in his love for others? What suffering so costly as the suffering endured by that unsheltered and unoffending head on the cross, when the oaths of the Roman soldier, the hootings of the Jewish rabble, the taunts and the scoffs of the priests, rose up and struck his ear, and when his eye could see alone of all his friends a woe-begone woman or two, and a solitary disciple. The agony he then underwent at such guilt, such weakness, such degradation, far exceeded his bodily pains, racking, and tearing, and destroying though they were, and constituted the price which, of his own accord, he paid for us and for our redemption; yea, for the redemption of the very men who were imbruing their hands in his innocent blood (1 Tim. ii. 6). Here is true honour gained by God's own Son, and here are claims which call forth from our heart the most fervent acknowledgments. Honour Christ all do and must who can any way feel his worth—honour him beyond, immeasurably beyond, the highest of earthly excellence. That honour I cherish, and resolved I am not to allow the honour to be dimmed by any philosophic refinements or theological profundities. Yours truly,

JOHN R. BEARD.

LETTER VI.—REASONS WHY I AM A UNITARIAN

(*Continued.*)

I AM A UNITARIAN BECAUSE UNITARIANISM IS, 13TH, DESTRUCTIVE OF SIN; 14TH, PROMOTIVE OF HOLINESS.

MY DEAR EDWARD,—13. *I am a Unitarian, because Unitarianism is Destructive of Sin.*—The common theology removes the punishment of sin, or leaves the sinner to suffer for ever The last is a wretched issue, especially when the fate awaits the great majority of God's so-called children. The former is a *delusion.* The penalty of sin is never removed until the sin is renounced, and not renounced only, but replaced by holiness; and holiness is not a gift but an acquirement. These are facts in God's government of the world. They are laws of Divine providence. They are declarations of the will of God, and so demand attention from all men, especially those who assume to teach others. Recognising the behests of the supreme will, Unitarianism aims at nothing short of destroying sin. Knowing that sin and well-being are as incompatible as disease and comfort, it makes the removal of sin its great work. Causes rather than consequences it regards, assured that the stream will be sweet if the fountain is pure.

Wise in its purpose and aim, Unitarianism is wise also in its means. No magical efficacy does it expect from without. For no sudden transformation does it labour. Ecstasies it fears rather than invites. In its judgment, the religion of the passions is as short-lived as Jonah's gourd. Owning, and gratefully employing, God's aid, it teaches *the art of self-cure.* Not content with saying *be strong*, it shows the way how to *become strong.* Following God's analogies, it extends a hand to the down-fallen, supplies a crutch to the infirm, smooths the way before the stumbling, furnishes babes with milk, and prepares meat for full-grown men. At the same time, it distinctly and emphatically declares—"Work out your own salvation, for the very reason that God worketh in you and with you." How does the broken leg become stout? First by medical skill and care, then by gentle exercise, and then by vigorous movements. In the same manner are the weak in the faith to be lifted up, that, by voluntary effort in God's vineyard, they may acquire strength, and health, and joy.

But the Gospel renews as well as heals. In order to cleanse the soul, it pours into it a fresh and limpid stream. In order to quicken its dormant energies, it bestows on it the elements of higher life. Such is the function of Christ. Christ destroys sin by infusing into the sinner his own energies. Thus light expels darkness when day dawns, and a joyous countenance makes every other face glad. A medieval superstition cured old age by filling its veins with young blood. The superstition veils a divine truth. If you would arrest moral decay, magnetise the spirit with new forces. The surest way to drive out a prejudice is to call forth a sympathy. You hate me? I will do you good, and so make you love me. Thus Christ himself is still ever overcoming our evil with his good. This is the spirit and this the power that removes mountains of sin, and that Christian community is nearest and dearest to Christ in which Christ's enkindling, reviving, and elevating efficacy is most felt, cherished, and exercised. That, in this particular, Unitarians are all that they might be, and all that they ought to be, I dare not affirm. But their principles it is which I now expound; nor is it a bad omen that they are not too proud to confess their actual deficiencies. I must add, that from them comes a large portion of the genial influence which is now purifying society by the streams of a considerate, sympathising, and uplifting benevolence.

14. *I am a Unitarian because Unitarianism is promotive of holiness.* The pecularity of Unitarianism is not so much that it brings man into immediate communion with God, as that the God with whom it brings man into communion is the one only God whose essence is paternal wisdom, authority, and love. Such relation shuts out all intermediaries save the Son of God, who, as having the spirit of God without measure, is God's sole ambassador and representative. Accordingly, it disallows sacerdotalism of every kind. When sacerdotalism disappears, all ritual service becomes impossible. Consequently, conscience is left alone with its own supreme paternal Source and Governor. Perfect religious freedom ensues as a direct and inevitable consequence. The spirit of man worships before the footstool of the one absolutely perfect Parent. In that Parent's will is man's law; from that Parent's hand he receives all good, and the sanctions to his virtues proceed from the same all-wise, all-powerful, and tenderly-loving Source. If God is holy, and if man is capable of holiness, holy such a worshipper must become, at least in the final issue; for the free worship of infinite parental goodness is simply the love of that goodness; and love invariably begets its like. Of no small moment is the concentration of spiritual forces here secured. But those forces of the human spirit are concentrated on The One Absolute Good. Still more, The One Absolute Good is adored and served by the worshipper as in the highest sense his Father. On the throne of the universe, then, he finds infallible wisdom for his guidance, inexhaustible goodness for his support, and boundless pity for his solace; while his fear and his hope are sustained and made perfect in their working, by an omnipotence

that can overwhelm, and a love that can redeem and save. Thus, the soul of each Unitarian is the centre toward which all the powers of heaven gravitate, and in which they meet, bringing with them all the light, succour, and sanction which the Father of the universe holds in his hands. Lest such splendour should prove overpowering, a human medium is interposed, who, on the one side presents the Father's glory in a tempered form, and on the other bestows sympathy and encouragement for his fellow-aspirants. Thus the Son is at once God's image and man's brotherly helper. The whole combines in light, power, example, and rescue, to make the perfect man in Christ. If religion has any force, here is that force at its maximum. What labour too great to gain the love of the "Father Almighty?" What spiritual attraction so strong as that Father's tenderness radiating from the face of his son Jesus Christ? What an overpowering consideration that the unutterable bliss of a Father's presence and the inconceivable woe of banishment therefrom, depend on my being or not being in symp thy with Christ. Now I feel that I have indeed to bear my own burden, while I also feel that infinite powers are at my side—shielding me, strengthening me, fighting for me. The fact is strikingly exemplified in the celestial messenger that brought succour and solace from the Father to the Son, when in his fearful agony he all but said, "Remove this cup from me" (Luke xxii. 42). Thus religion, without losing the august countenance and the sublime port of her celestial origin, enters our home, takes her seat at the hearth, and speaks to us in the touching and prevailing tone of parental authority. Becoming the chief of our domestic sanctities, she hallows and blesses our hearts individually, and transmutes our home into a miniature of heaven. Confessedly, home is the nursery and the abode of moral power and grace, and the form of religion which is most parental must be most productive of holiness. In its root-idea, Unitarianism fulfils the command which underlies not the Mosaic religion only, but religion itself—"Be ye holy, for I am holy."

Yours truly,

JOHN R. BEARD.

LETTER VII.—REASONS WHY I AM A UNITARIAN.

(Continued.)

MY DEAR EDWARD,—15. *I am a Unitarian because Unitarianism guards against polytheism on the one side, and pantheism on the other.* Polytheism, the doctrine which owns many gods, distributes the Divine, while pantheism, or all God, dissolves it into thin and impalpable air. One of the greatest services done to human kind by the Bible is the preservation of God as the Creator and Father of men. This it has done by its vigorous assertion of the one living God whose will is the fountain of universal life and happiness. The assertion is made not in any abstract form, but—far better—by the ceaseless presentation of the Creator, Father, Governor, and Saviour of men on the stage of visible existence. In some sense God is the sole agent of the Bible. From him come all things; in him all things consist; by him all things are guided; to him all things tend. His life is the life of the universe; his will is the source of law; his word is the light of the world. Independent of creation, he yet fills creation.

Above all, he is not the less in all. Self-subsistent, he is the fountain of being. Equally is he in the stream of being—the force and the hue of every drop.

Such a view of God satisfies our human thought, and so sustains itself. In sustaining itself it negatives its opposites, and its opposites are polytheism and pantheism. Polytheism it makes impossible, by fixing the human mind on the one creative will. Pantheism it makes impossible, by confining the human mind to the one intelligent centre. That will is so rigidly one as to refuse to be multiplied. That centre is so intensely concentrated as to refuse to be diffused. Happy resnlt! for polytheism ever tends to pantheism, and pantheism is nothing better than a luminous mist.

Here Unitarianism works powerfully on the side of the Bible. It sternly guards the one will against any usurpation. It sternly keeps the one centre against any dissipation. Its one God is really one, if only because he is a father. A father cannot, as a father, be more than one, nor can a father be a nebulous mass.

On the contrary, Trinitarianism ever tends to polytheism, with no small risk to end in pantheism. It ever tends to polytheism. There is but one branch of the entire Church in which Trinitarianism is what it was, retaining all the qualities of its fully developed form. That form is Roman Catholicism. Here, then, we may see Trinitarianism as in its perfect condition, so in its natural fruits. Accordingly here are "gods many, and lords many," not less than in the heathenism described by Paul. Besides the greater gods, the Roman pantheon is crowded with demi-gods, heroes, local gods, gods of nations, gods of individuals. To the long-recognised number of the greater gods, another has, in process of time, been added ; and, as in ancient days Zeus dethroned Chronos, so now Mary eclipses the three persons of the Trinity. Even in Protestant Trinitarianism a somewhat similar result is observed, for now the Father is practically supreme, and now the Son, while the Holy Ghost finds little beyond a nominal recognition.

Facts such as these can little satisfy the logical demands of philosophical speculation. Accordingly, in Germany, Trinitarianism has begotten pantheism, while pantheism adopts the nomenclature of Trinitarianism. What, in the mouths of Hegel and Strauss, is the Trinity but the passage of the subject into the object? The Father is the Infinite which, through the Holy Ghost, becomes the Son; while, reversely, the Son, through the Holy Ghost, returns into the Father. Thus life is transition. Thus the universe is change. Thus all is everything and everything is all. Sad to think that speculation, encouraged and aided by ecclesiastical falsities, should have resolved the grand biblical reality of one God into such aërial films.

Yet to an issue so direful tends every departure from the strict monotheism of the Bible. The statement is vouched for by the history of the Church. Not content with Scriptural simplicity, Greek speculators, aided by the slender forms of divinity to which they had from their cradles been used, and under the influence of which they could and did ascribe divinity to the slightest manifestation of what seemed to them divine, soon saw, in the perfections of Jesus, reason enough to give him the name of God, which they gave to so many inferior objects. The result was aided by exaggerated love and blind reverence. Then poetry came to throw its hues and images about the new divinity. By and by logic intervened, and, on its hard anvil, gave consistency and form to the divine birth. The deification of Christ potentially contained the

Athanasian Trinity. The first step down the steep declivity of theological speculation was set, and thenceforward descent was unavoidable, nor could it be stopped until the bottom was reached. Yet even in the vale there was a depth so deep as to require centuries to fathom ; nor has the lowest point been got to even by the Marian idolatry of the present hour, for why should not the Pope, who can place a divinity on the ecclesiastical Olympus, assure there a seat for himself?

Very jealous for the one God, the Father, ought all disciples of Christ to be. Oh that Unitarians understood the duty to which they are called. Let them feel the dignity of their work. Let them be faithful and vigilant watchmen on the walls of Zion. Neither without nor within the holy city let them tolerate any deviation from the truth of truths, the central fact of the universe, the one thought of the Bible, the sap and the life of every true human mind—namely, "There is one God, and none other but he." The moment that light is dimmed, darkness and corruption may enter the soul, bringing weakness and death in their train.

You, my young friend, I heartily congratulate, in that you are turning your mind to the great questions involved in the issue under consideration. The result I will not anticipate, for, though I hesitate not to express strongly what I feel strongly, I have no desire to exert any personal influence on your decision. May that decision be the work of God's Spirit in your soul.

Yours truly,

JOHN R. BEARD.

LETTER VIII.—REASONS WHY I AM A UNITARIAN.

(*Continued.*)

My Dear Edward,—The reasons set forth in the foregoing pages have made me a Unitarian. Indeed, I might select two or three of them—for instance, the intelligibility, reality, reasonableness, and Scripturalness of Unitarianism—as the influences which compel me to be a Unitarian. In this selection I should give prominence to the Scripturalness of Unitarianism. The Bible has been the study of my life. I am fully satisfied that the Bible is a Unitarian book. I have no doubt whatever, but the fullest assurance, that the mind of the Spirit of God, as declared in the sacred Scriptures, is unreservedly, fully, and clearly in agreement with the substance of what is termed Unitarianism. The Bible sets forth one God and one Lord. The one God it styles the Father, to the exclusion of all other beings. The one Lord it identifies with Jesus of Nazareth—himself one even as God is one. Further, the Bible teaches that God is love, and that the love of God is offered to man in the one Lord, who, in consequence, is the Saviour of the world. This, I say, is the one faith of the Bible; and this, as the one faith of the Bible, is the basis of Christian fellowship. This one faith is not a theology, but a revelation; not a conclusion wrought out by my own mind, but a disclosure made by God's Spirit. It is something which has come into me from the Source of light, and so has come out of the deepest places of my spirit. My part, however, has been not creation, but recognition and appropriation. The truth is God's; I do but see what he shows me, and the eye by which I see his truth he made capable of sight. Were Unitarianism with me a mere theoretical deduction, or a system of divinity constructed by myself, I would not retain it for an hour. No religion would it be to me; no guidance, no power, no life, o support could I expect from it. Made by man, it would deserve and share the fate of all things human, and probably be discarded by myself before I reached my grave.

You are, then, I must take leave to say, wrong in representing me as placing my reliance on "an earthly foundation." Equally are you wrong, and not a little inconsistent, in intimating that I am "too earnest to be tolerant." "Tolerant," indeed, I cannot be, for it is not my part to bear with you in your views as with something wrong. Differ from me you do, but not more than I differ from you; and, as I lay claim to no infallibility, so I have no right to impute certain and positive error to you. You intrepret the Scriptures in one way. I interpret them in another way. Differing in the result, we may be one in heart, and so ought to be one in charity; and one in heart we are, if we both love the truth, and do our best to come to the knowledge of the truth. To me, indeed, my interpretation is the right one. I can see only with my own eyes, and inasmuch as I have taken what appear to me the best means of gaining spiritual sight, and am not aware of any warping or darkening influence, at least of a marked character, I feel confident of having been led by God's spirit into God's truth. Nevertheless, I cannot identify my sight with actual realities, though to me those realities are contained in that sight. I say *to me*, wishing to mark the difference I acknowledge between truth as it is in the mind of God, and as it is in my mind. In this acknowledgment is the true ground for charity. And here I am met by a consideration which has no small influence in making me a Unitarian; for, needful as charity is to the genuine Christian life, I look for it in vain among the popular sects, where, indeed, even-handed justice, at least towards those who believe less than themselves, is, alas! very rare.

16. *I am a Unitarian because Unitarianism is unsectarian.* "Think and let think" is its motto. This true Christian principle it could not recognise, did it hold that salvation was by any form of opinion. Were salvation by any form of opinion, then, to me it must of course be my form of opinion And if I held that the acceptance of Unitarianism was indispensable to save you from perdition, I could not tolerate your ruinous error. At any rate, I ought to spare no effort which had the slightest chance of rescuing you, and those whom you might influence, from everlasting death. Hence would arise a zeal too burning to be charitable. Such is the zeal of most of our popular Churches, and such emphatically is the zeal of the Papacy. Very needful, therefore, is a zeal more according to knowledge. That zeal, having its foundation in a knowledge of the Bible, makes a sense of want, and not a string of theological conclusions, the condition of acceptance with God. That sense of want, inherent, in a greater or less degree, in all earnest natures, is specially fostered in the soul by the Spirit of God in Christ, and so abounds most where not a creed, but a sympathy, is made the bond of union between the soul and its Maker. This recognition I find in the Unitarian community, and in consequence I am glad to be one of its members. That sympathy may exist in two forms. It may be in a measure an unconscious sympathy. So was it probably in the case of the woman who washed Christ's feet with her tears, and wiped them with the hairs of her head. It may also be a conscious sympathy, as probably it was in Mary, and perhaps in Martha. When conscious it not only feels a want, but distinctly knows where to find a supply. The want

springs from a sight of infinite goodness. In the same pure and bottomless fountain is the supply found. In other words, the Father's love, as imaged in the Son's, is at once the occasion of the felt want and the source of its satisfaction. Here is a recognition—a conscious and practical recognition of God and Christ—all-sufficient for the great purposes of the religious life; for it is no vague recognition, as of Divine power; nor is it a blind recognition, as if a mere sentiment; but a knowledge of God in Christ, as the refuge and the safety of the soul. Such knowledge is what the Gospel describes and demands. The knowledge has two sides:—relatively to the theologies of the schools it knows nothing, and so is simply negative and excluding; relatively to the religion of Jesus, it means to be all that Jesus teaches, that it may obtain all that Jesus gives. And thus in its substance it is Unitarian, while beyond that substance it is not Trinitarian. Such knowledge is theological, inasmuch as (and no farther than) it includes an intelligent recognition of God and his Son. Such knowledge is religious, inasmuch as it is, under Divine influence, a birth into the higher, the divine life. Here is the true knowledge of the way of salvation—a knowledge which is accompanied by full assurance of faith, for if anything knows itself without mistake, it is moral goodness and power. Yet, with all the certainty attending this divinely-produced consciousness, there is no exclusiveness, but rather a belief that, as the ways of Infinitude are infinitely various, so God, dealing this way with me, may deal in another way with you; for the Saviour himself taught that the Spirit of God, in the regeneration of the soul, works as diversely, nay, as mysteriously, as the winds of heaven, which come no one knows whence, and go no one knows whither, producing effects which no one can explain (John iii. 8). This divinely authorised latitude of thought guarantees a corresponding largeness of heart which makes intolerance impossible. Where but in the Unitarian communion shall I look to find such latitude and such largeness? All my brother ministers may not agree in the view I have given of the cause of that latitude and largeness, but all to a man would, I am sure, subscribe to my teaching, that it is the duty of every Christian, and so of every Unitarian, not to condemn any truth-seeker under the pain of being condemned himself.

It is, however, a simple and undeniable fact that Unitarians are unsectarian. So unsectarian are they that some foolishly, almost superstitiously, fear sectarianism. I have known the fear close their lips, paralyse their hands, empty their places of worship, and famish their institutions. The fear is liable to periodical gusts. Ever and anon, within the last half-century, it has broken forth, and producing a desert, called it peace. All manner of guises does it assume, to all manner of subleties does it resort, in order to make the Christian disciple believe that he should not proclaim the truth that is in him, but sit and wait till some other truth comes—as if God's way to God's truth lay not in active and devoted fidelity to the light of the present hour. Or, if the fear allows the disciple to move and work at all, it plants a hedge around him, and says, "Hitherto, but no further." Associate with your fellow disciple you may, for your own individual benefit and solace, provided always the contact be not too close; but if you and others combine for the purpose of bearing the torch of Divine truth into the dark places of the land, take no designation, have no banner, own no rallying-point, lest you should sink from a Church into a sect, and compromise the future. Compromise the future! What can such a phrase mean in the Unitarian Church? By endowments you may try to fasten your opinions on posterity; but where, so much as among Unitarians, are endowments disliked and avoided? By stereotyping a creed, and fencing it round with blessings, cursings, privileges, and disqualifications, you may even do something to cramp and counteract the mind of the coming generation; but these arts are objects of aversion and attack, not of commendation, among Unitarians. Equally however may you injure your sons, and your sons' sons, by concealing the truth that is in you; by a timid, wavering, subservient, and worldly spirit; by any and everthing that conduces to indifference, mental torpor, ignorance, and moral infirmity; but never, and in no way, by out-speaking and plain speaking—by a manly avowal of your convictions—by an open and honest propagandism; for thereby you will not only strengthen your own nature, and cherish self-respect, but gain the esteem of all sincere and earnest men: and, by promoting healthful mental and moral activities, and at least endeavouring to advance truth and promote the Gospel, aid in giving birth to robuster minds, and nobler aims, and loftier and purer religious apprehensions. He who hides his own light does his best to keep his successor in darkness. Among the best of benefactors are those who, after due preparation, let their light shine before men, and even become as a city set on a hill, provided always that they so speak as that, in and through their efforts, men may glorify God.

Let every man and every age do the work that lies before them, and that asks their attention, and then they may safely leave the future to take care for itself. Sufficient for the day is the work thereof. But no man has a right to even speculate about the future who does not do his best for the present; and the best for the present is, always and in all things, and by no means least in religion a simple, open, straightforward, and vigorous declaration and maintenance of what seems to each one the truth. That truth may not be pure truth; certainly it will not be God's whole truth—enough that it is your truth; as your truth it demands your allegiance, and your allegiance, neither to your own truth nor to God's truth, can you show, unless by unreservedly contributing such light as you have to the common stock, and promoting, as far as you can, both by principle and example, free, full, and fair discussion; which is God's own appointed way to mental and moral life, health, strength, and continual growth. In regard to literary pursuits, who will question these statements? In collegiate studies, those who honour and exemplify them in their conduct, are classed with the great friends of their race. What, then! are these most beneficial and laudable endeavours to be suspected, feared, and disallowed, when the question is the proclamation of God's everlasting Gospel? Methinks I should like to see the righteous warmth with which Paul or John would sweep away such cobwebs, had an attempt been made to impede their free and manly steps as they went out to preach the Gospel to the world. And would that God's Spirit were now poured out on our Churches, in a fire so intense as to burn up all the fears and refinements by which its movements are hindered and its efficiency crippled. As a community of Christians, we are bound to promote the kingdom of God upon the earth; and the most efficient method to foster Church-life within our own borders, is to promote the Christian life beyond them. For this purpose, we must, as honest men, speak forth the word that is in us. That word is Unitarianism. Utter the word: if it is now dwarfed by want of utterance, it will, when outspoken, grow. Utter the word: if it is a word of man, it will perish, as it ought to do; but if it is a word of God, it will do God's work, and in doing God's work, bring back into our sanctuaries things for their enrichment and adornment more precious thad gold, and more lovely than rubies.

No, Edward, you need be under no apprehension of being sectarianised by approaching the Unitarians of England. Nor does the fear say much for your manliness; or if your manliness is right, can your knowledge be what it ought to be? Why, what is this bugbear? Innocent enough is the word sect. A sect is but a segment, that is, a part of some whole. Christianity was at the first a sect, and, as Unitarianism is now, "a sect everywhere spoken against." As the founder of that sect, Jesus was a sectarian; as its promoters, sectarians were all the apostles. Of all sectarians, Paul, Peter, and John were the greatest. That, however, which they espoused as a sect, they espoused so earnestly, that from a sect it grew to be a Church, and being the Church of one city, one country, it is going forward to be the Church of the world. How? By self-disregarding effort. The great souls of men, too full of the Spirit of the Father and of the Son to stop to draw hair-breadth distinctions, when thousands and tens of thousands were perishing for hunger, poured out their priceless treasures on social deserts, which straightway blossomed and bore fruit. Did those great souls wait for new light, when the old which they had was in their eyes so precious and so needed? Did they speculate about the future, or acknowledge the overpowering claims of the present? Did they trouble themselves about their position, and debate about their name? They were absorbed by higher considerations, and going out to work, *even as they were*, they received the Divine blessing in new light and fresh power. Labour for God resolves many a knotty point, and what it does not resolve, it brushes away, or leaves where it is, as too unworthy for serious notice—certainly, too inconsiderable to retard or embarrass the activities of service which God demands, and in which is the fountain of the true Christian life. Yet were those servants of God all of one mind,—of one name? Ulfilas, the Unitarian missionary, and Athanasius, the Trinitarian theologian, Vincent Saint Paul, urged by his Catholic love, and Tuckerman, impelled by his Unitarian benevolence, went out and preached the Gospel in God's highways, making many, very many hearts, no less glad than pure. They each worked in the line of direction in which they were called of God. There they worked, undeterred by any fond fear of being sectarian, and as little solicitous about their designation. Their perfect love cast out, or kept out, all small fears and all fine-drawn distinctions. This workman men called Arian, and that workman they called Trinitarian; this Catholic and that Protestant. No matter; without caring to disown the names, they meant to be Christians, and certainly were resolved to do a Christian work. Doing that work, they were kept by God in the genuine Christian spirit, and so were preserved from the unclean spirit of sectarianism. For, my dear friend, sectarianism lies not in the doctrine, still less in the labour, but in the motive and the aim. He that works for himself or his party, exclusively or mainly, is a sectarian, wherever he is, and however he is called. He that means to do God's work, and makes that work his desire and his object, is not a sectarian, but a servant of God, wherever he is, and however he is called. Trinitarian or Unitarian, Protestant or Catholic, no matter which or what, all serve Christ who sincerely strive to promote the cause of Christ, though, instead of calling themselves Christian, they bear the designation of the several communities with which they are connected. Equally may they be at work for themselves at the very time they bear and profess the name of Christ alone. Among the factions in the Church at Corinth, there was one whose adherents said,—"We are Christ's," and employed the honourable name so as to dishonour and disown its sacred interests. Our religious name is, indeed, scarcely more a matter of choice to ourselves than the name we receive at our birth. We come to our names as we come to our social positions. Diversity of operations in the Church necessitates diversity of names. The moment a dozen men associate together for a religious object, they are sure to receive a name from others, if they do not give themselves a name. That name to be descriptive must be distinctive, and it cannot be distinctive without becoming exclusive, and in becoming exclusive it may prove offensive. What then? The offence is not intentional; the service must be rendered, and so the indispensable conditions of the service must be accepted. If, to avoid the appearance of sectarianism, you shun all names, you will bring on yourself some name of reproach, or at least men will say you are ashamed of your opinions. If, under the same consideration, you try to discover or invent a name which is neither distinctive nor descriptive, you will do little else than raise a laugh at your own expense—well if you are not also charged with indifferentism or craven-heartedness.

If, in order to stand on the broadest possible basis, my associates and myself take the name of Christians, we lay ourselves open to the imputation of denying the Christianity of others, while our neighbours will probably punish what they think our presumption, by turning our name into a nickname; thus the numerous body of Unitarians in the United States who call themselves Christians are denominated *Christ-ians* by the world around them. In their anxiety to avoid a sectarian basis, other Unitarians have called themselves "Liberal Christians," and so gave their opponents occasion to charge them with narrowness and presumption, as if they thought themselves either the only "Liberal Christians," or "Liberal Christians" *par excellence*. The position is not improved if "Bible Christian," or "Free Church," is taken as your designation. Indeed, all this pother about names is very small. The name you bear may not be the best possible; but, since it is yours, however you came by it, let it answer its purpose, and, by honourable work, make it honourable.

From these remarks you will see that I have no sympathy with your objection to the name of Unitarian. Though not fond of any name but that of Christ, I shall retain the one I bear, at least until you or some one else provide me with a better. Meanwhile, I do the best I can with the name I have, if only because that is the sole way to any improvement. "If I were nearer to your views that I am, I should feel little disposed to take so obnoxious a name." These words are unworthy of you. Do you wish to re-enact the part of Nicodemus? The fear of men has more to do with your dislike than the love of truth. Discourage the temper that thinks to profit by the light, without bearing the penalty of its open avowal. Better remain where you are, than bring near our camp a coward's heart. The name Unitarian is a good name. It is descriptive. It has a definite meaning. It is recognised. Nay, it is authoritative—as far as authority is possible in the case. Any way it is too late to change it. As it is too late to change it, what but idle talk can come of objections made thereto? I will place under your eyes a few facts which will illustrate these statements.

From the words of Tertullian, quoted hereafter, words which were uttered in the second century, when the growing-up in the bosom of Christianity of Trinitarian notions called forth opposition thereto from the greater body of believers, we learn *

* Tert. Adv. Prax. Cap. 3.

that, in the collisions which ensued, the watchword of the majority was *unitas* (oneness), and the watchword of the minority was *trinitas* (trinity). From this word *unitas Unitarian* is naturally and regularly formed. Thus, a Unitarian is one who asserts God's unity or oneness, declaring him to be one being, strictly and properly, that is, one being in one person, in opposition to the then new and aggressive doctrine of the Trinity, by which its advocates, hence called *Trinitarians*, meant one God in three persons. I have intimated that the name Unitarian may be readily formed from the word *unitas*, which was the characteristic doctrine of the primitive disciples in general. That the name Unitarian was borne by them, history does not show. It is, however, probable that this designation was given to the Unitarians by their assailants. From their assailants came other names connected with them in the earliest ages. These were either names formed from the names of eminent Unitarians, or they were names which contained a gross misrepresentation of views which they held. To such appellations they could give no countenance. Nor, indeed, do they appear to have taken any name but such as was common to believers in Christ during some centuries. In the first ages they hardly did so, for, being then the majority, they would naturally continue to think and speak of themselves as Christians, and that denomination served for all practical purposes. And when the views they entertained were assailed by Tertullian and other innovators, and attempts were made to fasten on them names which either misrepresented their ideas, or made them followers of some distinguished teacher among themselves, they wisely refused to adopt the appellations, if only lest they should thereby compromise the position they took, namely, that they were, as from the first they had been, the great body of Christian disciples.

The reason, however, which may have made them refuse the inventions of their opponents—namely, that they might so serve God's truth, now in our altered condition, in which we have not to retain, but to recall and restore that truth, demands of us such an explicit, open, and manly profession of our faith as can consist only with our taking, bearing, and honouring a denomination which at once declares our doctrine, and marks how it is distinguished from the false theology of the Church. Such a denomination presents itself in the term Unitarian, which, as we have already seen, is the historical and appropriate opposite to the term Trinitarian. Born of the controversy forced on the Church by heathen and speculative theologies, the name Unitarian must be retained until its rival Trinitarian has received its death-blow; when we may fall back into the primeval unity, and worship the God and Father of the Lord Jesus Christ in the simplicity of loving and reverent hearts.

Another name is distinctly connected in history with the early Unitarians, which is too descriptive of their characteristic doctrine to be passed unnoticed. They are called in Tertullian, *Monarchists*, from the Greek *monos* "alone." This designation that writer gives them because, as he states, they maintained the Christian monarchy, that is, the government of one only God, the Father, in contradistinction to the government of more Gods than one, which they saw in the Trinity. The name is little else than the Latin term Unitarian in a Greek form. Whether the name originated with the primitive Unitarians or not, it is not easy to say, though I incline to the affirmative, but this is certain—namely, that if by the monarchy we understand the supremacy of the Father, then it may be taken as descriptive of the view held by the Christian Church in general during three hundred years after the birth of Christ; nor indeed would it be difficult to show that most of the distinguished advocates of the Trinity have in all ages admitted such a supremacy in the Father as may be ascribed to the source or fountain of the Godhead. Here is another undesigned testimony to Unitarianism, nor can that testimony cease to be borne so long as the God of Jesus is termed his Father in the New Testament.

The contrast and conflict called out in the second century, by the intrusion into the Church of Trinitarian tendencies of thought, came forth in a more distinctive and conscious form in the early days of the Lutheran Reformation, when worshippers of the one God, even the Father, who in Poland called themselves the Polish Brethren, expressly adopted in Hungary the name of Unitarians. This name appears in the title of a work which they put forth in Latin, containing an authoritative exposition of their faith. I translate the title as exactly as I can:—"A Summary of Universal Christian Theology, according to the Unitarians, composed and published for the use of Students of Divinity. Clausenberg, 1787." In the preface we are informed that the work contains, in Parts I. and II., "a general view of the religion or doctrine of the Unitarians, drawn from the fountains of Sacred Scripture themselves;" in Part III., "the rules and sanctions of an upright and pious course of Christian life, or Christian ethics, common to all who are Christians; and, in Part IV., "a picture of the Christian Church, with the connected topics." The "conclusion" of the summary is so excellent, as well as so characteristic of Unitarianism, that I cannot deny myself the pleasure of giving a translation of it:—"Christian reader and censor, this is and was the view and the theology of the Unitarians concerning the articles of the Christian religion; in and from which you may see that they refuse rashly to decide the not necessary matters—such as do not tend to promote the Divine glory, nor conduce to the edification of themselves or their neighbours ; you may also learn that they do not curiously search into those mysteries which are not revealed to men ; that they avoid unfruitful speculations (Tim. i. 4) : that they do not unnecessarily trouble their fellow-Christians with things indifferent, and external ceremonies, introduced by the Church; that they hold that those who differ from them, though they may be wrong in their opinions, are to be tolerated in mutual love, and to be commended to the mercy of God (2 Tim. ii. 24, 25, 26) ; and that they devote all their energies to this object—namely, to obtain and promote salutary truth, truth which it is the interest of all to be acquainted with, and which leads to solid piety, the salvation of individual men and women, and to universal peace and concord (Tit. iii. 8 ; Heb. xii. 14 ; Ephes. iv. 3 ; Phil. iii. 15, 16); therefore, actuated by fraternal love, do you not admit all kinds of accusations, calumnies, and detractions against them, or readily lend an ear to the words of those whose interest it is that the espousers of the Unitarian religion should be ill spoken of ; rather, if you think Unitarians err, instruct them in a spirit of gentleness, for they are ready to yield to those who show a more excellent way, and to divine truth, which is to them more precious than any other thing."

If an apology for the use and retention of the name Unitarian were wanting, it would be supplied in these admirable words. Ashamed of myself should I be were I ashamed of the spirit which breathes here ; and if this is Unitarianism, may I be as true to the reality as I hope to be to its designation. What, however, chiefly commends both, is, that both have been honoured in the lives of thousands who are not unworthy of being described as "the salt of the earth." In making this statement I come upon another of your derogatory remarks:—"After all, Unitarians have been but second-rate men." What Unitarians were in the early Church—what they were, what they thought, and what they did then and in the middle ages, neither you nor I can describe in particulars, if only because their antagonists not only did their worst to exterminate them by fraud and force, especially under the aid of the secular arm, but succeeded only too thoroughly in burning and destroying their writings, and almost all the monuments of their history. Even in England it is only within the last few years that the persecution which formerly wasted Unitarians with exile, fines, imprisonment, and the stake, has ceased its barbarous rage. "Second-rate men," say you? You pronounce their eulogy—for a eulogy, a high eulogy it is, to hold a second place amid the devastations to which Unitarians have been subjected, from the fourth century down to recent days. There is, however, a merit which places them among the great ones of the earth, and makes them dear in the sight of God:—a merit to which most professors are not a little blind. The persecutions through which Unitarians have passed, give them a glorious position among the confessors and martyrs of the Christian Church. All who, in any age—all, whatever their peculiar doctrines—who spoke out the truth that was in them, undeterred by rude ignorance or brutal force, are in the best sense of the term sons of God, and benefactors of their kind. These are the glory and the lights of the Church. They asserted the true dignity of the human mind, and the immeasurable worth of the Gospel; they maintained man's responsbility to the sole Lord of conscience; they vindicated the freedom, as of individuals, so of the Church. it was owing to their manly and righteous free-thinking that soundness and vigour survived in Christendom; else the corruption would have been universal, and from corruption rottenness would have been engendered, to have its consummation in moral darkness and death. Even if those whom the predominant party branded as heretics were wrong in logic, certainly they were right in spirit and purpose. In truth, however, they had, I believe, the better cause, as well as the nobler soul. Unless I have misread the lessons of ecclesiastical history, the heretics are the great men of the Church—not merely its spiritual heroes, but its lights; and so deep is this conviction, that my sympathies and my admiration are all but invariably with the losers rather than the winners in the great and ever-recurring combat of the spirit of truth against the spirit of error.

I am no Arian, but I think more highly of Arius than of his successful opponent Athanasius; toward Pelagianism my views do incline, but I respect the name of the old confessor of Brittany (whatever country that was), not because he was right, but because he was ill-used. The struggling Luther would possess my heart had he failed in his grand enterprise, while all the grandeur of Leo X. is insufficient to reconcile me to the abominations of his court and the falsities of his religion. Mental ability is indeed a "good gift," but little to be respected is power, unless when employed on the side of God and humanity. The skill of Calvin as a Biblical commentator only makes his compassing the death of Servetus a greater crime: for it goes far to exclude the extenuating plea of ignorance, and was of little real worth if it did not enable him to surmount the ruthless spirit of his age, as it was surmounted by other men of the day, scarcely less able than the Genevese Reformer, and more imbued with the Spirit of Christ. It is the possession of that Spirit which should conciliate the esteem of Christ's disciples, even as it is that on which rests the favour of God, and from which comes the good of society. Can this be questioned, when it is manifest that not the favourites, but the victims of the world are its principal benefactors, albeit their names are cast out as vile? Were not the apostles counted as the offscouring of all things? Was not Christ crucified for blasphemy and treason? And what judgment did the venerable and beloved sufferer pronounce in this issue?—"Woe unto you when all men speak well of you!" "Blessed are the persecuted!" All God's highest servants spoken of in the Bible, are men of small mark, if judged by ordinary human measures, and equally were they all traduced, overborne, or put to death. Who so brilliant in ability and position as David and Solomon? and who more degraded? Who so humble in rank and estate as "the prophets," in whom God placed his Spirit? and who so evilly entreated? Surely you cannot have studied the Bible with due care and earnestness, else how could you have missed one of its greatest lessons, to the effect that God works out his sovereign will by instruments that are of small account in the eyes of men. The death of Christ sums up and shows forth God's method of salvation in social as well as religious life. It is only by the cross that men can be lifted out of the dust.

The spirit of the cross lives in the Unitarians of the present hour. They are not, indeed, all they ought to be. I am not blind to our shortcomings. On suitable occasions, I have not failed to set them forth, with the blame they seemed to deserve. The rather may I be now pardoned if I declare that the body contains a class of men of whom history will one day say, that, in a period of transition, they moved with their age, while they carried with them, as Israel of old, the ark which symbolised at once the truth and the presence of God; that in an adverse state of the public mind, they proclaimed what they believed to be the everlasting Gospel, in patience and hope preparing brighter days for their successors; and that in order that they might be faithful to the work they had received at the hands of Providence, they struggled on, with very narrow means, in the midst of opulent or substantial circles, and gained respect and esteem from good and intelligent men of all denominations, notwithstanding the intense prejudice against their faith prevalent in the popular mind. This class of men bear the name of Unitarian ministers. May the class, whatever improvement they may make, never forfeit one jot of their mental culture, nor lose aught of their sterling integrity!

I have shown you that the name Unitarian is distinctive, and as such appropriate. I have shown you that it was deliberately adopted by the Unitarian Church of Transylvania, which may be described as the mother of British and Transatlantic Unitarians. It is, moreover, a fact that the designation has been formally taken by individuals and bodies, among both the British and the Transatlantic Unitarians of mark, sufficient to give influence, if not authority, to their act. Another fact important in the matter is, that Unitarian has become the acknowledged designation of our communion, having all but entirely superseded "Socinian," to which we objected, because it denoted us as disciples of a fellow-man, Socinus, and having displaced "Presbyterian," which has hardly even an historical reason for its employment. At a time when things are quietly settling down into a general acquiescence in the name Unitarian, you, especially as you are not within our pale, come somewhat too late with your objections, and practically will have to decide either not to take Unitarianism at all, or to take it with the appendage of a received and suitable designation. How entirely this is the sole practical alternative, appears from the fact that the word

Unitarian is used by the dictionaries as the proper designation of members of our Church. Several instances lie around me. I confine myself to two. Dr Fleming, in the recently published second edition of his instructive "Vocabulary of Philosophy," uses (p. 542) these words:—"A Unitarian is a believer in one God. It is the same in meaning as a monotheist. The name is commonly opposed to Trinitarian, and is applied to those who, accepting the Christian revelation, believe in God as existing in one person, and acknowledge Jesus Christ as his messenger to men." A fuller and better account is given by Dr. Ogilvie in "The Imperial Dictionary" (1851):—"The Unitarians are a sect of religionists who confine the glory and attribute of divinity (deity it should be) to the one only great and supreme God and Father of our Lord Jesus Christ. The Unitarians are opposed to the Trinitarians, or those who conceive of one God in three persons, characters, or relations, each of which they regard as the proper object of religious worship. The Unitarian Christian believes the Father to be the only true God, and Jesus, his messenger, to be the Christ. This is the leading fundamental principle which constitutes the true and complete definition of the term Unitarian, under which are consequently included all those who, receiving the divine authority or commission of Jesus Christ, believe him to be a dependent creature, deriving his existence from tho Father, and, therefore, the fit object of all the veneration, submission, and obedience which can be offered to a creature, but none of religious worship, properly so called. Agreeing in this great and leading principle, Unitarians differ in their opinions as to the origin, nature, and dignity of Jesus Christ. One division of them has received the name of Arians, another that of Socinians."

Yours truly,

JOHN R. BEARD.

LETTER IX.—REASONS WHY I AM A UNITARIAN.

(Continued.)

My Dear Edward,—17. *I am a Unitarian because Unitarianism, being propitious to peace and union, is the nucleus of the one universal Church.* Orthodoxy has occasioned in the universe three great gulfs :—1, a gulf between the Creator and the Creation ; 2, a gulf between the Father and his children ; and, 3, a gulf between different portions of those children These several gulfs, which make peace and union impossible, Unitarianism fills up, uniting the sundered parts by the idea of the one universal Father, who sends his Son to be the Saviour of the whole world.

Orthodoxy is dualistic as well as trinitarian. With it matter is something, if not independent of God, yet impenetrable to God. Borrowing the old Greek idea of a certain primaeval stuff, out of which God is fabled to have made the world, it recognises in *nature* a sort of inferior divinity, and so is the source of the scepticism which deifies human generalisations under the name of laws. Accordingly, between God and nature, there is, in the popular mind, alienation and repugnancy. Nature withstands God ; God tries to subdue nature. The conflict, proceeding from the outward to the inward, goes on in the human mind. Hence the natural is more or less the sinful. Accordingly, the spirit of man is all but impervious to the Spirit of God. Its movements, until impregnated with overpowering grace, are low, sensual, and devilish—objects of God's wrath and sources of man's woe.

This dualism reaches its height, and takes a personal form in Satan, who, like God, has his kingdom and his ministers. Between God and Satan there is perpetual war. The war involves, on the part of God, the loss of the love and obedience of all his human family. A remnant is rescued from the dominion of sin and the devil by Christ. Satan, however, is the master of the great bulk of human-kind, and will hold and torture them for ever. Thus our race is broken and divided into two masses—the smaller mass is God's, the larger mass is the devil's. The sunderance extends from time throughout eternity.

Here are the three gulfs of which I spoke:—the gulf between the Creator and the creation, the gulf between the Father and his children, the gulf between different portions of those children. The fatal dualism, inherent in the substance of things, is interminable. Until two are one, orthodoxy cannot produce unity and peace in God's universe.

Here the special value of Unitarianism comes into view. One God, the Creator and Father of all, has one abiding-place, the universe, which is simply the manifestation of himself. In that universe all forces are divine, all tendencies are divine, all results are divine, when regarded in their origin, aim, and final issue. The laws of nature, then, are God in action. Consequently, whatever is natural is good. So did God pronounce all the works of his hands good at his first great creative act. Thus every natural function, affection, movement, and effort is good. To eat is good. To sleep is good. To labour is good. A mother's love is good. Good also is the youth's passion. Marriage is good. I mean, that, in themselves considered, these things are good. Other considerations intervene. If you eat when you are full, you commit a sin, and are punished. You have a moral nature as well as an animal one. The laws of your moral nature carry with them their ow sanctions. They *will* be obeyed. Hence you are compelled to say, "I ought," "I must." Obedience to that necessity is good.

God, then, in its highest character, arises at the point where the claims of the animal and the claims of the moral nature are blended and harmonised. Hence sin arises in their divergence and opposition. Consequently, sin is disobedience to your highest law. That law is conscience. Conscience is Go working in man's soul. If, then, you obey conscience, you obey God, and so are at one not with yourself alone, but with your Creator. If you disobey conscience, you disobey God, and so are at variance with God and with yourself. Here arises the only divergence possible in God's universe. Man's will, as being free to choose, may rebel. Rebellion is sin, and sin is death. But physical death is only passing into life. Hence we may believe that, under the Government of an Omnipotent Father, moral death is not the final doom of any intelligent creature. Meanwhile, all such creatures are God's children; they wear his likeness; they are fed by his hand; they are watched over by his Providence; they are led by his Spirit; they are redeemed by his Son. With diverse gifts, and in diverse positions, they are all men, and all alike objects of the same paternal care. They have one nature, one duty, one destiny. The world, then, is a nursery; God's government is patriarchal, and heaven is a home; or rather, heaven is the home for which earth is the school. The realisation of these grand ideas is "the unity of the spirit in the bond of peace," of which Paul speaks, and on which he so often dwells with special delight. (Eph. ii. 14; iv. 3; Col. iii. 14; 1 Cor. xii. 12.) Of this universal union, the Son of God is the focal point. He makes perfect and perpetual peace, not merely by uniting Jew and Gentile, but by bringing man's will into complete and abiding harmony with God's. He who, in virtue of his filial piety, became the Son of God, raises every true follower into a share of his own sonship, and so makes him one with God.

The final result is, that God is all in all. The Spirit of the blessed Father beats in and actuates the spirit of every child. (John xvii. 15, *seq.*)

Such is Unitarian Christianity in its highest and widest reaches and issues. To Unitarianise society, is to bring about universal peace in heaven and on earth. It is to fulfil, in the deepest sense, the prayer taught by the Saviour, and whispered even by infant lips—"Thy will be done on earth, as it is in heaven." That prayer shows forth the deepest desire of Christ's heart. To work for the realisation of that desire, is surely the noblest employment of the powers we have received in trust from our Heavenly Father.

And now you will see that Unitarianism is the true and proper centre of the one Universal church. The fact admits of several illustrations; but here I confine myself to the train of remark in which we have been engaged. Unitarianism is the embodiment of the one true unity, since it is the recognition of the one true God. This recognition has love for its essence—the love of the infinite Father to his finite child, the love of the finite child to his infinite Father. (Mark xii. 29—33.) Owning the one Father, and the one Son, Unitarianism is the nucleus of the one Church—consisting, and to consist, of all who serve the Son and adore the Father. This gathering-point—the loving service of God in Christ—is as simple as it is true, and as attractive as it is simple. Already is it acknowledged in the deep heart of Christendom. Daily is the acknowledgment becoming more conscious and more open. In order to its continued progression, disciples of Christ have only to cast away adventitious and uncongenial accretions; while the humanity and comprehensiveness of its spirit is making for it a way into unbelieving minds and heathen lands, with a promise of universal diffusion. Of such a spirit, orthodoxy is a poor and insufficient channel. Yet, since even orthodoxy carries the Sacred Scriptures wherever it goes, and contains the essence of Unitarianism shrouded in its own creeds, so orthodoxy is unconsciously doing a Unitarian work, carrying forward a Unitarian propagandism, and promoting God's own unchangeable and everlasting truth.

Yours truly,

JOHN R. BEARD.

LETTER X.—REASONS WHY I AM A UNITARIAN.

(Continued.)

MY DEAR EDWARD,—18. *I am a Unitarian because Unitarianism is sufficient.* It is sufficient, I mean, for all the purposes and all the issues of actual life. How, indeed, can it be otherwise? What more can we have? What more can men want than a God who is a Father, and a Saviour who is at once the Son of God and a brother man? If God is really your Father, are you not God's child? and, if you are God's child, what good thing can you lack, whether for this world or for the world to come? And when I say Father, I mean such a Father as is pictured in Christ his son. Can Trinitarianism do more for you than secure the mercy and love of omnipotence, or bring you nearer to God than you may be in virtue of a vital union with Christ? Clearly, the peculiar doctrines of Trinitarianism are so much surplusage, for they cannot do more for you than can be done for you by the God and Father of the Lord Jesus Christ. You say "I am a sinner"—was not Jesus sent to save sinners, and of those who came to him did he send any away unforgiven and unblessed? You tell me, "I labour and am heavy laden,"—then, why not listen to the gracious invitation which Jesus continues to utter to such as you, "Come unto me all ye who labour and are heavy laden, and I will give you rest"? You write, "I am uneasy and distrest in thought of the future,"—did not Jesus come "to deliver those who through fear of death, were all their lifetime subject to bondage"? You continue, "I fear the last dread account,"—then, in the spirit of a disciple's love, give a cup of cold water to a disciple, and verily you will not lose your reward. You argue, "I cannot think that anything I can do will merit the divine favour." Assuredly not; but the humility of that assurance is the very state of mind in view of which God will, of his own free and spontaneous benignity, bestow the grace which he sent his Son to offer to the world. You declare that God must punish sin; and I reply that, while God punishes sin, he is ever at work to renew and save the sinner. You are sure that you cannot satisfy God's law; and I reply that God's law is satisfied, when its purposes and end are secured in the destruction of the evil power which causes its transgression, and in the reformation of the heart of the transgressor. You argue that you want an expiatory sacrifice, by which God may be reconciled to you; and I reply that the death of Christ is God's propitiation, designed to win you over and reconcile you to himself. I add, further, that your uneasiness, your fears, your factitious wants, spring mainly from your ignorance and infirmities. Oh! if you only accepted, simply and gratefully accepted, God's offered goodness and all-sufficient grace, if you only believed in God as the Father of Jesus and as your Father; if you only knew Christ as Christ is visibly set before your eyes; if you were only free from the darkening, distorting, distracting influences of systems of false divinity; if you could only realise your true position as God's own child, whom he loves more than we love an only son, and yearns after more than we yearn after a long absent daughter, and pities more than we pity our erring and wandering brethren, and ever seeks to rescue, to lift up, to purify, make holy and happy, more than a Howard pitied the prisoner, or a Clarkson the slave—then your unreal alarms would cease, your troubles would be composed, your darkness would vanish, and you would be at peace in the bosom of God, as the infant is at peace in the bosom of her who gave it birth and loves it best.

"We are told, indeed, that our faith will not prove an anchor in the last hour. But we have known those whose departure it has brightened; and our experience of its power in trial and peril has proved it to be equal to all the wants of human nature. We doubt not, to its sincere followers, death will be a transition to the calm, pure, joyful mansions prepared by Christ for his disciples. There we expect to meet the great and good Deliverer. With the eye of faith we already see him looking round with celestial love on all of every name who have imbibed his Spirit. His Spirit, his loyal and entire devotion to the will of his heavenly Father, his universal and unconquerable benevolence, through which he freely gave from his pierced side his blood, his life, for the salvation of the world—his divine love, and not creeds, and names, and forms, will there be found to attract his supreme regard. This spirit we trust to see in multitudes of every sect and name; and we trust, too, that they who now approach us will at that day recognise in the dreaded Unitarian this only badge of Christ, and bid him welcome to the joy of our common Lord."—*Channing.*

Yours truly,

JOHN R. BEARD.

LETTER XI.—REASONS WHY I AM A UNITARIAN.

(Continued).

My Dear Edward,—19. *I am a Unitarian because I believe that Unitarianism is important.* How important Unitarianism is in my judgment, I have no words fit to declare. To me Unitarianism is the Gospel, and the Gospel is God's grace for the extirpation of sin and the redemption of the world.

I regard the Gospel as the great panacea of human woes. Nor is the good it bestows merely negative. The Gospel aims to make every man perfect, and perfect even as Christ is perfect. The design and tendency of the Gospel is to bring peace on earth, good-will to men, in such a way and to such an extent as that the issue may be glory to God in the highest degree, and unto all eternity. In one word, the design and tendency of the Gospel is to universalise the spirit, the power, the blessedness of Christ, and so to make God all in all. Nothing less than these majestic results is what the God, who is the Father of all men, especially of those who believe in his Son, and seek and foster his spirit, is at this very moment desiring, and longing, and working to bring about. How poor a word is "important" with which to characterise results so grand, so comprehensive, so enduring. As fellow-workers with God for these divine achievements, most willingly do I recognise all sincere disciples of the common Master, to whatever denomination of Christians they may belong. Among those true and devoted followers of Christ, are many who profess some form of Trinitarianism. Not in that form, but in the religion which lies under that form, and which that form is unable to suppress, do I recognise the fountain of their light and power, while it is the firm and abiding faith of my heart that the same religious essence which constitutes the substance of Unitarianism, is the very object which God approves and loves in their spirits, and on which he sends down the softening and enriching dews of his blessing. Nor can I for one moment doubt that the great design and object of the heavenly Father is to Unitarianise, first, the Church, and then the world. Already does the history of the past show to me, by unmistakable signs and proofs, that Unitarianism, in the shape, first, of patriarchal monotheism, then of Mosaic monotheism, and then of Christian monotheism, is the instrument designed and employed of God for working out the highest good of his intelligent creation. Monotheistic are all the principal religions of the past. Monotheistic are all the highest forms of civilisation. Every form of existing civilisation is high just in the degree in which it is monotheistic. Monotheistic are all the greatest civilising agents, operations, and tendencies of the present day. England is great because it is so largely monotheistic. Monotheistic is its best literature. Monotheistic are its noblest spirits. The purest currents of its religion are monotheistic. These monotheistic powers and tendencies, are too, more or less Christian in spirit, and so form an element in that unconscious Unitarianism which is the substratum of the Church.

Yours truly,

JOHN R. BEARD.

LETTER XII.—REASONS WHY I AM A UNITARIAN.

(Concluded.)

MY DEAR EDWARD,—20. *I am a Unitarian because Unitarianism being the most ancient faith of Christendom, connects its disciples immediately with Christ.* If, as I have shown,

Unitarianism is the doctrine of the Bible, then Unitarianism must have been the earliest form of the religion of Jesus. That earliest form appears in the New Testament. Let us come down below the limits of the Scripture, and ascertain in what form, Unitarian or Trinitarian, the religion of Jesus now appears. I do not propose to descend later than the second century, because I am concerned only with the most ancient faith of Christendom. If we ascertain what was the doctrine of the first two centuries, we thereby decide what was the most ancient faith of Christendom. Let me further premise, that the words reported as having been uttered by our Lord, when on the point of ascending to his Heavenly Father, namely,— "Go and make disciples of all nations, baptizing them into the name of the Father, of the Son, and of the Holy Spirit" (Matt. xxviii. 19), and which contain a summary of the essential points of Christian instruction and belief, form the connecting link between the doctrine of the Apostolic Church, and the doctrine of the post-Apostolic Church. In these words there is a criterion enabling us to distinguish between Unitarianism and Trinitarianism. The application of the criterion is made clear by reference to usages which came in and obtained prevalence in later ages. These usages consisted in the addition of certain terms, the object of which was to define metaphysically the nature ascribable to each of the three subjects—the Father, the Son, the Holy Spirit—and then to determine the relation which they severally bore the one to the other. In the earliest times, no traces of such an attempt are discernible. When first such an attempt makes its appearance, it is only partially and dimly. Growing by degrees, the effort appears in an advanced state in the creed put forth in the Council of Nice, in the year A.D. 325.

Out of this form was gradually developed the full and proper form of the doctrine of the Trinity, which finds embodiment in the creed which is falsely ascribed to Athanasius, but which seems to have come into existence not earlier than the eighth century of our era. These facts exhibit Trinitarianism to you as a growth, and not only as a growth, but a product of the Church. The product is the outcome of Pagan speculation, dealing with the great spiritual ideas of the Gospel, so as to harden and compress them into forms congenial with its own logical and systematising tendencies and habits. Thus God's Word, which is life, was petrified into man's notions, which change and perish. Mark, I beg of you, what it is which this philosophising spirit undertook to do. It undertook to put on Scriptural terms, meanings which the Scripture itself did not put on them. Thus it added to Scripture, and it so added to Scripture as to make the import of Scripture not only more definite, but more restricted. "Our sense," it said, "is the only true sense." Thus an orthodoxy was fabricated, expressly intended to expound and supplement Scriptural truth. Men, fresh from the school of Plato, were not content to accept the New Testament in all its divinely-given simplicity, largeness, and comprehensiveness, nor would they accept it at all, unless when dressed up in the phraseology with which education had made them familiar. In a word, Christ was attired in the raiment of speculative philosophies, and then preached as the only true Christ. A fatal error was this, if only because it forced on the religion of the Bible a spirit totally different from its own, and so prepared the way for the deadly corruptions of the Papacy. "Science, falsely so called," found the religion of Jesus a sublime spiritual life, and left it a corpse. Such ever is, and ever must be, the tendency of all attempts on the part of speculative intellects to give systematic form and colour to the everlasting verities of the Bible, which possess all the simple grandeur of the mind of Christ, are an image of the mind of God, and so are wholly incapable of improvement. When men attempt to recast God's truth in the moulds of their own systems of what they call philosophy, they unavoidably reduce the infinite to their own small dimensions, and in the process press out its life and distort its features.

Three principal steps in this downward progress are open to your inspection in the book of Common Prayer. The first is, what is termed the Apostles' Creed; the second, the Nicene Creed; the third, the Creed of Saint Athanasius. Here you observe the evil growth in the main stages of its progress. The creed bearing the name of the Apostles, was not composed till long after the Apostles themselves were dead. Formed piecemeal through a succession of years, it marks the first step in the wrong direction—namely, the step which assumed that the truth, spirit, and power which made the essence of the Gospel, could be compressed and embodied in a formulary of combined doctrine and history. This incarceration of the Christ of God, led to his petrification, as begun in the Nicene Creed, and completed in the Athanasian. Before I pass on, I must beg you to study the first form of Christian confession with some attention. As being nearer to the apostolic age, it retains much of its simplicity and amplitude. You may, indeed, graft Trinitarianism on it, but you cannot get Trinitarianism out of it. I shall set before you yet simpler images of the faith of the first ages.

The command to baptize converts in the name of the Father, and of the Son, and of the Holy Ghost, ascribed by Matthew to Jesus, was observed in the days of the Apostles by baptism in the name of "Jesus Christ" (Acts vi. 38, 41), or in the name of "the Lord Jesus Christ" (Acts viii. 16; xix. 5), on the simple confession, "I believe that Jesus Christ is the Son of God" (Acts viii. 37). This fact, which we learn from the Book of Acts, shows that no special importance was attached to a trinal form, as must have been the case had a three-fold gate been the sole entrance into the Church. However, the requiring of a profession of faith in Christ, and the employment of some form in baptism, gave speculators an opportunity for fabricating, multiplying, and enforcing creeds. Next in antiquity to the simple acknowledgment of Jesus as the Christ or the Son of God, was the profession of the Father, Son, and Holy Spirit as the chief topics of Christian instruction. In process of time other objects of belief were added, so as to form a creed, and in corrupt days the principal of those received metaphysical definition. Thus the primitive faith, passing through the alembic of speculation, was transmuted from the pure gold of religion and history into the silver and brass of scholastic determinations.

The earliest form of what is now called the Apostles' Creed, in other words, the earliest confession of the primitive Church, after the simple acknowledgment of the Lord Jesus Christ, in which was implicitly contained all true Christianity, was

The Creed of the Church of Alexandria in Egypt.

"I believe in the only true God, the Father, the Almighty:
And in his only begotten Son, Jesus Christ, our Lord and Saviour:
And in the Holy Spirit, the life-giver."*

I subjoin other forms of the same early period.

The Creed of the Roman Church.

"I believe in God Almighty:
And in Jesus Christ his Son, the only begotten,

* These creeds are given in their original state. See Bunsen's "Christianity and Mankind," vol. vii. p. 91, *seq.*

who was born of the Holy Spirit, and of Mary the virgin,
who was crucified under Pontius Pilate and buried,
and on the third day rose from the dead,
ascended into heaven, and sat down on the right hand of the Father;
whence he comes to judge the living and the dead:
And in the Holy Spirit;
the holy church;
the resurrection of the flesh;
the life everlasting."

The Oriental Creed.

"I believe in one God, the Father Almighty:
And in one Lord, Jesus Christ, his only Son,
who was born of the Holy Spirit and the Virgin Mary,
was crucified under Pontius Pilate, and buried,
the third day he rose from the dead,
ascended into heaven,
sits at the right hand of the Father,
thence he is about to come to judge the living and the dead:
And in the Holy Spirit;
the holy church;
the remission of sins;
the resurrection of the flesh."

Several other similar forms lie before me;* but, as they are little else than repetitions, I abstain from translating them. In order that you may have before your eyes the additions made by the council of Nice, I translate its creed from the original Greek.

* "Bibliothek der Symbole," &c. By Dr. A. Hahn, Breslau, 1842.

The Nicene Creed.

"We believe in one God, the Father Almighty, maker of all things, both seen and unseen:

And in one Lord Jesus Christ, the Son of God himself, the only begotten of the Father, that is, the essence of the Father, God of God, light of light, true God of true God, begotten, not made, of the same substance as the Father, through whom were (or were made) all things, both things in heaven and things in earth, who for us men and for our salvation came down and was made flesh and was made man, suffered and rose on the third day, and went up into the heavens, and is coming to judge the living and the dead:

And in one Holy Spirit."

Even this form of doctrine is Unitarian. Observe that the one God is declared to be the Father, and this one God, the Father, is pronounced to be Almighty. The same is not said of the Son. On the contrary, the Son is described as God of (in the Greek it is *out of*) God, that is God begotten of the Father. Accordingly, the Father is the source of the divinity of the Son. If so, the Father alone is God supremely; in other words, the Father alone is God in the proper sense of the term.

Observe, too, that whatever is said of the Son, he is not declared to be either equal or one with the Father, but is described as the instrument through whom all things were made by the Father. Observe, again, that the Holy Spirit is left, in all its scriptural bareness and simplicity, unqualified and unsupplemented by ecclesiastical authority. Finally, observe that the creed lays down nothing regarding the three in their aggregate form. In other words, the Trinity is passed over in silence.

Here, however, you have in a marked degree the unhappy propensity to dogmatical definitions, which is the source of the rank corruptions of later days. Those ill-omened words, *that is*, point to the source of that infatuation of the sacerdotal and monkish mind which, resting on the assumption that God's truth was heresy, unless accompanied with human definitions and supplements, filled the Church with formulas of man-made opinion, and either hid or superseded the simple and sublime teachings of the sacred Scripture.

The first decided step toward a dogmatical and Trinitarian definition of Christianity is marked by that loss of charity which is the loss of the very spirit of the Gospel, and which, in its subsequent excesses, employed fire and sword to assert and defend Papal and Protestant orthodoxy. For to the Nicene creed, as given above, there is added this anathematising clause—"The universal Church curses those who say that there was a time when the Son was not, and that he was not before he was born, and that he was (or was made) out of things that were not, or assert that he was of a different hypostasis or essence, or that he was created, changed, or altered." This unbrotherly, not to say inhuman spirit, was accompanied by a lying spirit, for it is emphatically false to say that the decision of a majority of the Council of Nice was a decision of the Church universal.

Before I leave the point, I beg you to compare the so-called baptismal formula given in Matthew's Gospel, first, with the Nicene Creed, and then with the earlier forms of doctrine, as previously given, and you will need nothing else to show you that, even down to the year A.D. 325, the Church had not renounced the essential type of its own primitive Unitarianism, and that the more you go back to the apostolic age, the more simple is the form in which its Unitarianism appears.

I will supply one or two additional illustrations of these facts. How simply Unitarian is this very ancient

MORNING HYMN.

Every day will I bless thee,
And I will praise thy name for ever;
Yea, for ever and ever.
Vouchsafe, O Lord, to keep us this day, also, without sin.
Blessed be thou, O Lord, the God of our fathers,
And praised and glorified be thy name, for evermore.

Nor less purely and emphatically Unitarian is this primitive

EVENING HYMN.

Ye, children, praise the Lord,
Praise the name of the Lord.
We praise thee, we hymn thee, we bless thee,
For thy great glory,
O Lord and King, the Father of Christ—
The spotless Lamb, who takes away the sins of the world.
To thee belongs praise,
To thee belongs the song,
To thee, God and Father, belongs glory,
Through thy Son, in the all-holy Spirit,
To the ages of ages.

If now I subjoin a form of the thought uttered in the last hymn, in which corruptions of later growth appear, you will see another example of the downward tendency which reached its lowest point in the pseudo-athanasian creed.

Glory in the highest to God,
And upon earth peace, among men good-will.
We laud thee, we bless thee, we worship thee;
We thank thee for thy great glory,
O Lord and heavenly King, God the Father Almighty,
Lord, who art God.

Lord, the only begotten Son,
Jesus Christ.
Lamb of God,
Son of the Father,
Who takest away the sins of the world,
Pity us;
Who takest away the sins of the world,
Pity us, RECEIVE OUR PRAYER,
Thou who sittest on the right hand of the Father,
Pity us;
For thou alone art holy;
Thou art the only Lord;
O Jesus Christ;
To the glory of God, the Father.

Even this corrupt hymn, as it shuts up all "to the glory of God the Father," is essentially Unitarian. But it lets us see one principal source whence Trinitarian corruptions flowed—namely, the hymns of the ancient Church; for the praises and requests which were at first mere utterances to Christ of reverent and grateful hearts, grew and hardened in time into the full materialisms of the creeds, and thus the language of love and devoutness passed into the logical determinations of systematic divinity. The greater need is there that we should now utter in our hymns of praise no word which can encourage a departure from the strict and proper monotheism of the Bible.

The documents hitherto adduced set before you the established professions and worship of the Church. You see that it was Unitarian. Unitarian was it to such an extent that it did not cease to be so even in the Council of Nice. I have space for only one additional testimony. Tertullian, the distinguished Latin Father, gives the following as a statement of the general doctrine of the Church in his day:—

"There is only one rule of faith; single, unchangeable, irreformable; that which teaches belief in one sole God, the Almighty maker of the world; and his Son Jesus Christ, born of the Virgin Mary, crucified under Pontius Pilate, risen the third day from the dead, received into heaven, sitting now at the right hand of the Father, about to come to judge the living and the dead."

This, too, is simply a Unitarian creed, and this, according to Tertullian, was the faith universal in the second century. It is true that Tertullian somewhat draws out this statement, in another part, when describing the universal faith; but in that description he does not comprise a belief in the doctrine of the Trinity. It is also true that, when writing against the Unitarian Praxeas, he says that, "we believe this one sole God under the dispensation which we call the economy," alluding to a rudimental form of Trinitarianism, which he did much to introduce and establish; but this ecomony he does not describe as universally held, but claims it as the special privilege of the better taught, who had received the light from the Paraclete—a claim which sufficiently marks the recentness of the doctrine, and exhibits it as a result not of apostolic teaching, but of (alleged) special illumination. Tertullian is among the earliest of those who have been too proud of their literary and intellectual superiority to be satisfied with the teachings of fishermen, headed by a tentmaker and a carpenter. However, in complete agreement with his tacit, indirect, and undesigned admission that his doctrine of the trinal economy was not the doctrine of the universal church, he makes the following statements:—

"The simple-minded, not to say the unintelligent and doltish, which is always the greater part of believers, since the rule of the faith transfers them from the many gods of the (pagan) world to the one only true God, not understanding that he is indeed to be acknowledged as one, but one together with his economy, are alarmed at the economy. The number and division of the trinity they account a division of the unity, though the unity, deriving the trinity from itself, is not destroyed, but administered by it. In consequence, they publicly maintain that two and three Gods are preached by us, and presume that they are the worshippers of the one God, as if the unity irrationally apprehended did not amount to heresy, and as if the trinity rationally considered did not constitute truth. The monarchy, say they, we hold, and the word, even the Latins (though ignorant of Greek), yea, the hand labourers, utter so emphatically, that one would think they understood the monarchy as well as they pronounce it.* But while the Latins study how to pronounce the monarchy, even the Greeks are unwilling to understand the economy." †

This passage contains the following facts illustrative of the condition of the church in the second century, in regard to the respective doctrines of the unity and the trinity:—

1. The persons spoken of are the greater part of the disciples of Christ. These persons are comparatively of humble position and little culture.

2. They have been led to renounce polytheism by considerations which made them believers in the one only true God. This, the one only true God, did not involve the trinity.

3. The trinity is offered to their acceptance. It is a novelty. The trinity, in consequence, appears to the major part of the disciples of Christ in the second century as a novelty. It follows that Unitarianism was to them anterior to Trinitarianism.

* A sarcasm against the imperfect articulation of a Greek term by persons of Latin blood in humble life.

† Tertulliani adversus Praxeam, cap. 3.

4. When they have the Trinity before their eyes they become alarmed at it, and immediately set themselves in active opposition against the novelty, charging it with introducing three Gods.

5. In order the more explicitly and effectually to maintain their distinctive doctrine, they gave it a name, that name is the monarchy. The defence of the monarchy is, with them, the defence of the unity. On the other side, Tertullian puts forward, in opposition, the economy. The defence of the economy is the defence of the trinity. To the defence of the two, not only against the greater part of the believers, but against an eminent Unitarian, Praxeas, the learned, the rhetorical theologian, dedicates one entire work. Alarmed at the tendency of similar efforts, the Unitarians are zealous for the supremacy, nay the sole deity, of the one only true God.

6. With a view to gain his point, Tertullian utters reproaches on those against whom he writes. Scarcely are they worthy of his well-burnished literary sword. The Latin dolts want an elocution-master, and the Greek idiots are slow at a syllogism. A plain proof of a bad cause is this contemptuous abuse. However, evil is the servant of good, and falsity of truth, and so Tertullian has let it out that of both the Greek and the Latin Church, that is the Church at large, the greater number were in his day Unitarians, earnest and zealous for the grand central truth of the Bible.

7. From the description given of the Primitive Unitarians, it is obvious that they formed the great body of the Church. Now, the lower strata of society are the least given to change. The fact is too well known to require illustration. It follows from the fact, that the great body of the Church must have been Unitarian for some two or three generations. But two or three generations, reckoned from the time of Tertullian,

(born in Carthage about 160 A.D.), take us back to the days of, at least, the Apostle John. Tertullian's statements, then, place us in the apostolic age. They further show us the immediate results of the apostolic preaching; and if—as no one will deny—the apostles, in this momentous matter, taught as they were taught of Christ, the statements of Tertullian set before our eyes the effects of the teaching of Christ himself, and so give us at least the substance of his instructions.

8. How completely the faith which Tertullian assails was Unitarian may be further illustrated from the circumstance that he reproaches it with being a Judaic monotheism, as in these words—"It is a species of Judaism to believe in one God, so as to refuse to add to him, first, the Son, and then the Spirit." (Chapter xxxi.) Unhappily, the writings of Praxeas, together with all Unitarian literature from his day down to the Reformation, have been destroyed; but if we may imagine the reply that was given to Tertullian, it would be one of which no believer in God's revealed truth need be ashamed, whatever one may think of the spirit of an assailant who strove to profit by the prejudice felt in social life against the Jews, as having in their veins the blood of those whom the Scripture describes as the murderers of Christ. Beyond a question, the Mosaic religion is inferior to the Gospel, yet was it great and good enough to produce the Gospel. And if a thing is bad because Jewish, Jesus himself must be condemned or slightly valued. And surely it is a presumption in favour of Unitarianism that it leans upon the Jewish Church, the pillar of revealed truth for at least fifteen hundred years; and is by no means, as in Trinitarianism, in alliance with pagan speculation, to correct which was, and is, one of the great objects of the mission of Christ.

You have now seen reason to believe that Unitarianism was

the earliest form of the religion of Jesus. If so, then it was the religion of Jesus, for it was not only held by the primitive disciples, but taught by the heralds whom Jesus commissioned, and so presumably was the religion which they received from his lips and his life. Thus, even the assailants of Unitarianism as well as the liturgical services of the primitive Church, take us back, and, as do the Scriptures, place us face to face with the Son of God himself—the whole combining to enable us to sit at the Great Teacher's feet and learn of him. What more can be either done or desired? I say, then, that Unitarianism is the Gospel, because not only is it the earliest form of the Gospel, but, being so, it conducts us into the presence of Him who was, is, and ever will be, the Way, the Truth, and the Life.

These, my dear Edward, are the principal reasons why I am a Unitarian. I ask you to consider them, to consider them severally and conjointly, to consider them with earnest prayer to God for light and guidance. Should you be strengthened in the inclination shown in your last letter, be entreated to continue your studies; and, for that purpose, I subjoin the titles of some works in which you may find assistance. If you feel disposed to turn away from the matter, do not, I earnestly beg you, declare finally against Unitarianism, until you have carefully studied the Sacred Scriptures, in order to learn what God offers to teach you therein. Confident I am that the central thought of the Bible is Unitarian. In saying this, I do not mean that any merely intellectual assent comes up to what the Bible requires. The religion of the Bible is given of God to lead men to himself. The religion of the Bible, therefore, requires and demands in every man a holy life, as the outgrowth and fruit of a holy heart. You must be holy in heart if you would be holy in life. Without holiness you cannot serve a holy God acceptably. True holiness comes from God, the source of holiness. It is God's gift, conditional on our earnest and persevering endeavours. Make it your aim then to live a holy life. That aim should include worship as well as work. You must ask if you would receive. You must love religion if you would make it fully and permanently your own. And as, from your own confession, you have in your affections and in your conduct much that is contrary to the spirit and the precepts of Christ, much that is condemned by your own conscience, much that beclouds and confuses your mind and troubles your heart, much that makes your faith dim and weak, and sometimes almost shuts out God and heaven from your apprehension, you must, my dear Edward—yes, you must, ask God fervently and ceaselessly to give you his Holy Spirit, that you may be truly born from above, and, with a thorough renewal and sanctification of your inner life, become as a little child in the hands of your heavenly Father, who, when once you have surrendered yourself wholly to his influence, will make you not only pure, as Christ is pure, but trustful, contented, calm, and gentle within, and without useful—largely and increasingly useful—in promoting his own wise and benignant plans for the improvement of society, and, finally, for the salvation of the world. A better wish I cannot, in conclusion, utter, than that you may be put into full possession of the light, which is the true life now, and life for evermore.

Yours, in faith, hope, and love,

JOHN R. BEARD.

Woodfall and Kinder, Printers, Milford Lane, Strand, London, W.C.

Religious and Theological Works,

BY

JOHN R. BEARD, D.D.

THE HISTORICAL EVIDENCES OF CHRISTIANITY UNASSAILABLE; in answer to the Rev. Robert Taylor and Mr. Richard Carlile. 8vo, 1826.

SERMONS DESIGNED TO BE USED IN FAMILIES. Edited by John R. Beard. 8vo, Vol. I. 1829.

——— Second Edition, with suitable Prayers. 8vo, 1830.

A FAMILY PRAYER BOOK. 8vo, 1830.

SERMONS DESIGNED TO BE USED IN FAMILIES. Reprinted in Boston, United States. 8vo, 1831.

SERMONS DESIGNED TO BE USED IN FAMILIES. 8vo, Vol. II. 1831.

THE RELIGION OF JESUS DEFENDED FROM THE ASSAULTS OF OWENISM. 12mo, 1837.

A COLLECTION OF HYMNS FOR PUBLIC AND PRIVATE WORSHIP. By exclusively Unitarian Authors. 12mo, 1837.

VOICES OF THE CHURCH; in Reply to Dr. D. F. Strauss. 8vo, 1845.

UNITARIANISM EXHIBITED IN ITS ACTUAL CONDITION. 8vo, 1846.

HISTORICAL AND ARTISTIC ILLUSTRATIONS OF THE TRINITY. 8vo, 1846.

THE PEOPLE'S DICTIONARY OF THE BIBLE, with Maps and numerous Woodcuts. Several Editions. 2 Vols. 8vo, 1847.

The same, with additional Illustrations, &c., under the title of

THE HOUSEHOLD ILLUSTRATED BIBLICAL CYCLOPÆDIA. McPhun & Co., Glasgow. 1 Vol. 4to, 1865.

A BIBLICAL READING BOOK, containing a Life of Christ, for Schools and Families. 12mo, 1848.

——— Second Edition. 1849.

A BIBLICAL ATLAS. 8vo, 1849.

ILLUSTRATIONS OF THE DIVINE IN CHRISTIANITY. 8vo, 1849.

A CRITICAL HISTORY OF RATIONALISM IN GERMANY, from the French of Pasteur A. Saintes. 8vo, 1849.

AN INTRODUCTION TO THE BOOKS OF THE OLD AND NEW TESTAMENT, from the German of A. Schumann. 8vo, 1849.

A BIBLICAL PRIMER, in the Words of Scripture. 12mo, 1850.

THE GROUNDS AND OBJECTS OF RELIGIOUS KNOWLEDGE. 2 Vols. 8vo, 1856.

SABBATH LEISURE; or, RELIGIOUS RECREATIONS. In Prose and Verse. 8vo, 1857.

MAN'S ORIGIN, DUTY, AND DESTINY. 12mo, 1857.

A REVISED ENGLISH BIBLE: THE WANT OF THE CHURCH, AND THE DEMAND OF THE AGE. 8vo, 1857.

THE CONFESSIONAL: A VIEW OF ROMANISM. 8vo, 1859.

REASONS WHY I AM A UNITARIAN. 8vo, 1860.

——— Third Edition, British and Foreign Unitarian Association, price 2*s.* 6*d.*, 1872.

HYMNS FOR THE PUBLIC SERVICES OF THE CHURCH OF CHRIST. 12mo, price 3*s.*, 1860.

——— 24mo, price 1*s.* 6*d.*, 1862.

THE PROGRESS OF RELIGIOUS THOUGHT, AS ILLUSTRATED IN THE PROTESTANT CHURCH OF FRANCE. 8vo, price 5*s.*, 1861.

THE CHRISTIAN YEAR: A SERVICE BOOK FOR PUBLIC WORSHIP, compiled from the Bible. 8vo, 1861.

A MANUAL OF RELIGIOUS INSTRUCTION, from the French of Dr. Réville. 8vo, 1862.

THE HANDBOOK OF FAMILY DEVOTION, from the German of Heinrich Zschokke's "Stunden der Andacht" (Devotional Meditations), the favourite Manual of the late Prince Albert. 8vo, 1862.

THE LIFE AND WRITINGS OF THEODORE PARKER, from the French of Dr. Réville. 8vo, 1865.

CHRIST THE INTERPRETER OF SCRIPTURE, showing how to read the Bible wisely and profitably, with a Preliminary Essay on the Sources and Guarantees of the Gospel History. 8vo, 1865.

DISCOURSES ON THE CHRISTIAN MINISTRY, forming A Memorial to the Memorial Hall. 8vo, 1866.

A MANUAL OF CHRISTIAN EVIDENCE, containing as an Antidote to Current Materialistic Tendencies, particularly as found in the Writings of Ernest Renan, an Outline of the Manifestation of God in the Bible, in Providence, in History, in the Universe, and in the Lord and Saviour, Jesus Christ. 8vo, 1868.

THE AUTOBIOGRAPHY OF SATAN, with Illustrations. Williams and Norgate, London; crown 8vo, in cloth, 7*s*. 6*d*.

Works in General Literature,

BY

JOHN R. BEARD, D.D.

THE VISITOR OF THE POOR, from the French of Baron Degerando. 8vo, 1833.

AN ILLUSTRATED ITINERARY OF THE COUNTY OF LANCASTER, by Cyrus Redding, Esq., and John R. Beard. 4to, 1842.

*LATIN MADE EASY. Ninth Edition. 12mo, 3*s.* 6*d.*, 1848.

*A KEY TO LATIN MADE EASY. 12mo, 1*s.* 6*d.*, 1853.

THE PEOPLE'S BIOGRAPHICAL DICTIONARY. 2 Vols. 12mo, 5*s.*, 1851.

VOICES FROM CAPTIVITY. 8vo, 1852.

THE EVENING BOOK. 12mo, 1852.

THE LIFE OF TOUSSAINT L'OUVERTURE. 8vo, 1853.

CASSELL'S LESSONS IN ENGLISH, 12mo, 3*s.*		Reprinted in volumes from "The Popular Educator."
——— LATIN, „ 3*s.*		
——— KEY TO, 1*s.* 6*d.*		
——— GREEK „ 4*s.*		

Several Editions.

*CASSELL'S LATIN DICTIONARY, in Two Parts:—1, Latin-English; 2, English-Latin. By J. R. Beard, D.D., and Charles Beard, B.A. 8vo, 8*s.*, 1854.

——— School Edition. 3*s.* 6*d.*

MANUALS FOR THE SELF-TAUGHT:—

1. SELF-CULTURE; or, WHAT TO LEARN, HOW TO LEARN, WHEN TO LEARN. 8vo, 5*s.*, 1859.

2. THE RATIONAL PRIMER; or, "HOW CAN I LEARN TO READ?" 8vo, 6*d.*, 1860.

3. AN EASY INTRODUCTION TO THE ART OF LETTER WRITING, comprising, together with a series of Original Models, Instructions in English Grammar, and Composition. 8vo, 6*d.*, 1860.

Works marked thus * may still be procured through Messrs. Simpkin, Marshall, and Co., or Messrs. Cassell, Petter, and Galpin, London.

CPSIA information can be obtained
at www.ICGtesting.com
Printed in the USA
LVHW112023030423
743357LV00006B/744

9 783382 133481